THE WINTER PONY

ALSO BY IAIN LAWRENCE

The Giant-Slayer
The Séance
Gemini Summer
B for Buster
The Lightkeeper's Daughter
Lord of the Nutcracker Men
Ghost Boy

THE CURSE OF THE JOLLY STONE TRILOGY
The Convicts
The Cannibals
The Castaways

THE HIGH SEAS TRILOGY
The Wreckers
The Smugglers
The Buccaneers

THE WINTER PONY

IAIN LAWRENCE

DELACORTE PRESS

Text copyright © 2011 by Iain Lawrence
Jacket art copyright © 2011 by Tim O'Brien
Map copyright © Rick Britton

Visit us on the Web! www.randomhouse.com/kids

Educators and librarians, for a variety of teaching tools, visit us at
www.randomhouse.com/teachers

Library of Congress Cataloging-in-Publication Data
Lawrence, Iain
The winter pony / Iain Lawrence. — 1st ed.
p. cm.
Summary: An account—from the point of view of a pony—of what it was like to
be part of Captain Robert Scott's 1910 expedition to reach the South Pole
before rival Roald Amundsen.
ISBN 978-0-385-73377-9 (hc : alk. paper) — ISBN 978-0-375-98361-0 (ebook) —
ISBN 978-0-385-90394-3 (glb : alk. paper)
1. British Antarctic ("Terra Nova") Expedition (1910–1913)—Fiction. [1. British
Antarctic ("Terra Nova") Expedition (1910–1913)—Fiction. 2. Ponies—Fiction.
3. Explorers—Fiction. 4. South Pole—Discovery and exploration—Fiction.
5. Antarctica—Discovery and exploration—Fiction.] I. Title.
PZ7.L43545Wi 2011
[Fic]—dc22
2010053550

The text of this book is set in 12-point Goudy.

Book design by Kenny Holcomb

Printed in the United States of America

10 9 8 7 6 5 4 3 2 1

First Edition

WITH LOVE,
FOR MY FATHER

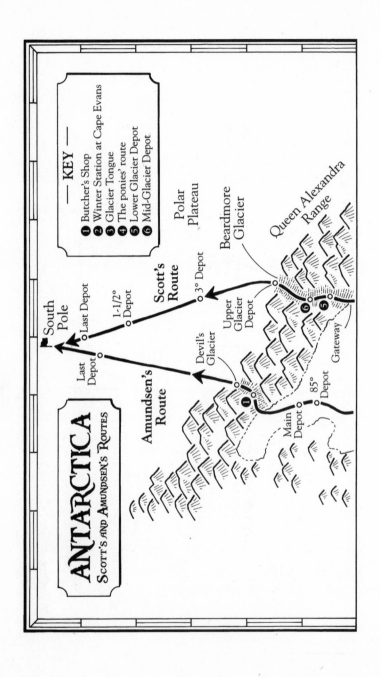

ANTARCTICA
Scott's and Amundsen's Routes

— KEY —

1. Butcher's Shop
2. Winter Station at Cape Evans
3. Glacier Tongue
4. The ponies' route
5. Lower Glacier Depot
6. Mid-Glacier Depot

Polar Plateau

Beardmore Glacier

Queen Alexandra Range

South Pole

Last Depot

1-1/2° Depot

3° Depot

Scott's Route

Upper Glacier Depot

Devil's Glacier

Last Depot

Amundsen's Route

Gateway

85° Depot

Main Depot

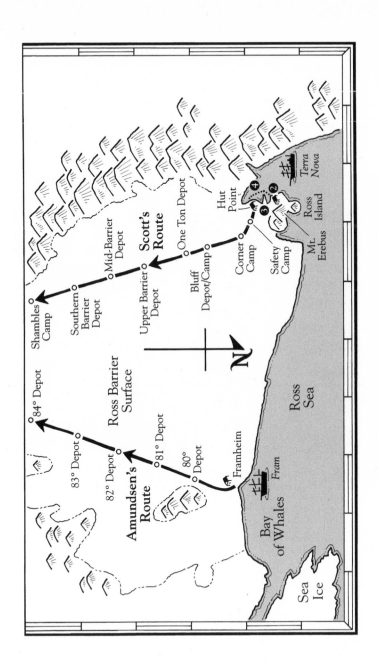

The year is 1910, and a great adventure is beginning. It will take two years to finish and will end in a desperate race across the bottom of the world, with a dead man being the winner. But for now it's just an adventure.

The American explorers Robert Peary and Frederick Cook are both home from the Arctic, each claiming to have beaten the other to the North Pole. There is now only one land unexplored, one place to discover: the South Pole. Men in six countries are raising expeditions in the hope of being the first to get there.

Two are nearly ready.

In London, Robert Falcon Scott is preparing a ship. He's a captain in the Royal Navy, already a hero of southern exploration. Seven years ago, with Ernest Shackleton and Bill Wilson as companions, he discovered the polar plateau and pushed his way past 82 degrees south latitude, about five hundred miles from the Pole. No one had ever been nearer.

There's a strong feeling in England that a Briton should be first to the South Pole. Donations pour in to Captain Scott's expedition. Eight thousand men volunteer to go with him. Lawrence Oates, a cavalry officer in the Inniskilling Dragoons, gives a thousand pounds in the hope that he can go along to care for the ponies that have been bought by donations from sailors. A young biologist named Apsley Cherry-Garrard is nearly blind without his glasses, but he donates another thousand to join up with Captain Scott. Schoolchildren raise money to buy sled dogs. Captain Scott himself travels up and down the country giving lectures and lantern-slide shows.

In Norway, the explorer Roald Amundsen is planning his own expedition. But he's keeping it a secret. He's telling his financiers that he means to go north, to study the Arctic Ocean by drifting with the pack ice. He hasn't even told his crew where they're really heading in his borrowed ship, the famous Fram. It would make no difference; they would follow him anywhere. Amundsen was the first man through the Northwest Passage. He has driven sled dogs across the Arctic and learned the ways of the Inuit. He was first mate on the nightmarish voyage of the Belgica, trapped so long in the southern sea that his companions lost their minds.

Both Scott and Amundsen know the frozen continent. Each wants very badly to be the first man to reach the South Pole.

It's an enormous prize they're after. It's fame and respect, a place in history. But what a trial to win it!

To reach the Pole, you have to navigate a frozen sea that only opens late in summer. You have to push your way through broken floes that might close around you at any moment and trap your ship forever, or crush it in an instant. When at last you get to shore, you still have nearly a thousand miles to travel, around the crevasses of the Great Ice Barrier, over mountains of staggering height, across a vast wasteland where enormous waves of snow are driven along by the wind. You can't carry all the food and equipment you'll need, so you lay depots along the route, trekking far to the south and back again, moving supplies forward. Then you build a shelter on the shore and sit out the southern winter, with temperatures to sixty below and darkness that lasts for months. As soon as spring appears, you're off to the Pole. You have to reach it—and return— in one long dash. You must be back before winter catches you in the open, before your food runs out, before your feet and fingers freeze.

If you're lucky, your ship might be waiting. There might still be time to get off the continent before the sea freezes again. But if you're late, or winter's early, you have to wait for another summer.

There are seals and penguins to eat, though many men choose not to. Everything else is brought in your ship: food for men and animals; sledges; harnesses; skis and boots and winter clothing. There's not a single tree on the whole continent, so you have to bring enough wood to build your hut, enough fuel to cook every meal.

You're in the loneliest place on earth. But there are signs here and there that others have come before you. A whole ship lies at the bottom of the sea, splintered by the ice. A wooden hut sits above the beach, food and sleeping bags still frozen inside. The walls of a stone shelter crumble by the shore. Tattered remains of abandoned tents blow in the wind like the clothes of old scarecrows. And little cairns of snow still stand on the dreadful Barrier, though the wind whittles them away, month by month.

You might wonder if it's worth the trouble, all the danger and the fear. But if you're the right sort of person, the answer is easy. All you can think about is that prize, the honor of being first to the Pole. So many men want it, but only one can have it.

Amundsen is taking nearly a hundred dogs. He believes they can pull light sledges all the way to the Pole. He means to move quickly, taking little food and few supplies.

Captain Scott is planning a lengthy stay and a careful assault. He's taking scientists to study the ice and the weather, the geology, the plants and animals. He's bringing motor sledges to carry the load for the polar party. He saw them in action in Norway and was so impressed that he now has three of the machines. Each can haul a thousand pounds at seven miles an hour, on and on, with no need for food or sleep.

He's taking harnesses for man-hauling, the British way of polar travel. But he's taking dogs as well, though he's afraid they'll let him down. On his last expedition, he had great trouble with his dogs and had to kill them all. Now he sends a man to Siberia to buy the best he can find.

Scott knows that Ernest Shackleton had greater success with ponies on his later expedition. So he instructs his man to pick out twenty ponies once the dogs are gathered. They must be light colored, every one, he says. All of Shackleton's dark-colored ponies died.

The man is Cecil Meares, an expert on dog teams and sledding. But he knows almost nothing about ponies. So he hires a Russian jockey to help, and they set out for the Great Wall of China, to a horse fair in the town of Harbin. He goes searching for Manchurian ponies.

CHAPTER ONE

I was born in the forest, at the foot of the mountains, in a meadow I knew as the grassy place. The first thing I saw was the sun shining red through the trees, and seven shaggy animals grazing on their shadows.

They were ponies. And I was a pony, my legs as weak as saplings. My mother had to nudge me to my feet the first time she fed me. But within a day, our little band was on the move. I skipped along at my mother's side, thinking I was already as fast and strong as any other pony, not knowing that the others had slowed to keep me near.

Our leader was a silvery stallion, as wary as an owl. We never crossed an open slope without him going first, standing dead still at the edge while he watched for wolves and mountain lions. He was always last to drink and last to graze, keeping guard until we'd finished. Except for one dark patch on his chest, his whole body was the color of snow. I loved to see him in the wind and the sun, with his white mane blown into shimmering streamers.

We had a route that took a year to travel, from the snow-filled valleys of winter to summer's high meadows. It brought us back every spring to a stony creek that we crossed single file. Our hooves made a lovely chuckling sound on the rocks as the water gurgled round our ankles. We climbed the bank on the other side, passed through a fringe of forest, and came to the grassy place, which I imagined to be the center of the world.

I thought everything would stay the same forever, that I would always be young and free, that day would follow day and the summers would pass by the thousands.

But even in my first year, I saw the young ponies growing older, and I saw an old one die. She was a big strong mare in the spring. But quite suddenly in the fall, she began to walk very slowly, to lag behind the herd. She didn't complain, and she didn't cry out for the rest of us to wait. She just eased herself away, and one night she wandered off to a watering place, all by herself in the darkness, and she lay down and didn't get up. I saw her in the morning, her nose just touching the frozen water, her legs splayed out like an insect's. I nudged her with my lips and found her cold and stiff, as though her body had become a stone. At that moment, I knew that nothing lived forever, that one day even I would die.

That was hard to understand. What did it mean to die? The grass didn't mind to be eaten, and the water didn't care if I drank it. But rabbits screamed when foxes pounced, and tiny mice shrieked for help as they dangled in eagles' talons. So why did the mare lie down so quietly, with no more grief or struggle than a fallen tree?

It scared me to think about it, and I was glad when the leader called me away. Across the valley, wolves were already howling the news of a fresh meal. So we hurried from there, off at a gallop through the forest. When wolves came hunting, ponies fled. We went on across a hillside, through a valley and up again, and we didn't stop until we reached the grassy place.

The next morning was exactly like my very first on earth. The sun was red again, throwing shafts of light between the branches. The ponies were scattered across the meadow, their shaggy manes hanging round their ears as they grazed on the sweet grass.

When we heard the clatter of hooves in the stream, we all looked up together. My mother had green stems drooping from each side of her mouth. The leader turned his head, his ears twitching.

At the edge of the meadow, a crow suddenly burst from a tree. I stared at the place, wondering what had frightened the bird. And out from the forest, with a shout and a cry, came four black horses with men on their backs. They came at a gallop, bounding across the clearing, hooves making thunderous beats that shook through the ground.

I had never seen a man. I had never seen a horse. I thought each pair was a single animal, a two-headed monster charging toward me.

My mother called out as she bolted. She reached the forest in two long bounds and vanished among the trees, still shrieking for me to follow. But I was too afraid to move, and the other ponies nearly bowled me over in their rush for the forest. Only the stallion stayed. He faced the four horses and reared up on his hind legs, seeming to me as tall as a tree. He flailed with his hooves, ready to take on all of the monsters at once.

They closed around him. The riders shouted. The black horses whinnied and snorted. They pranced through the grass in high, skittish steps, as though trampling foxes. And the stallion towered above them all with his silvery mane tossing this way and that.

Then one of the riders whirled away and came tearing toward me. His horse was running flat out, flinging up mud and grass from its hooves.

I cried for my mother, but she couldn't help me. I raced for the trees faster than I'd ever run before. I left the stallion to his dreadful battle and fled blindly for the forest. I heard the strange shouts of the men, the snorts of their horses, and thought that each monster had two voices. Amid their babble were the shrill cries of the stallion, full of anger and fear, and the frantic calls of my mother fading into the forest.

I followed her cries. I crashed through the bushes and wove between the trees, dashing through a hollow, hurdling a fallen pine. I stumbled, got up, and ran again. I dodged to the left; I dodged to the right, aware all the time that the monster was behind me. I could hear its deep panting and its weird cries, and the crack-crack-crack of a leather whip.

I came to the foot of a long hill. For a moment, I saw the herd of ponies above me, my mother among them, their white shapes galloping ghostly between the trees. And then a loop of rope fell over my head, and it snapped tight around my neck. I tumbled forward, my head wrenched right around until I thought my neck was broken. I lay on the ground, half strangled and breathless, as the monster glared at me with its four eyes.

I couldn't make sense of what I was seeing as the creature seemed to break in two. The man heaved himself up, then down from the saddle, and I realized the horse was much like a pony, just bigger and blacker. Without a word from the man—all by itself—the horse stepped backward to keep the rope taut around my neck. It kept staring right at me with a cold look, unconcerned by my pain. I didn't struggle; it was all I could do to keep breathing. I watched the man come walking toward me, and I wondered what sort of creature he was, that he could turn horse against pony so completely.

The men took me far away, half dragging me most of the time. I cried for my mother again and again, but it did no good. They took me down from the mountains, out of the forest, into a land full of people. They put me into a building as dark as a cave, into a narrow slot made of wooden fences. There were no more meadows and no more rivers for me. I drank from a rusted pail that gave my water a bitter taste. Once a day, a canvas bucket was shoved over my mouth and tied to my head, and I slobbered up the handful of grain that lay at the bottom.

Every morning, I was dragged outside, into a muddy corral. There I was broken. I was tamed and harnessed, then taught how to serve men. I learned to pull heavy weights, to obey commands that were always shouted at me. If I wasn't quick enough, I was struck with a stick or a whip or a fist. Once I was hit with a bottle, again and again, until it shattered against my collarbone. Every day was the same. The lessons lasted for hours, until the men grew tired of beating me.

To go from a life in a forest to a life like that made me sad. I wanted to drink from a stream, not a bucket. I wanted to run on the hillsides, to lie in the grass. I couldn't turn around in my stall, and I certainly couldn't lie down.

There was a whole row of ponies in the building, each pushed into its own slot, and among them—somewhere that I couldn't see—was the silver stallion. I often heard him snort and whinny. Sometimes he kicked at the fences, smashing the wood, and men came barging into the building. There were awful sounds then: cracking whips; shouts of men; the hideous scream of a pony.

I didn't like to hear that sound, and I let my mind wander away. Most of the time, it went back to the forest, to summer meadows, and I heard the whine of the black flies and the swishing of our tails. But one day, it wandered away to a different place altogether.

I saw a land of snow and ice, a gate so huge that its posts were mountains, its arch a curve of clouds. I saw it shining in the sunlight, the ice a glorious field of sparkles.

My mind didn't take me through the gate. But I somehow knew what lay beyond it: a place for ponies. I knew that the old mare from my herd was there, and all the others that had died before I was born. I told myself that I would go there one day if I was lucky enough to get through the gateway, and if I did, I'd find my mother waiting.

This wasn't a frightening vision at all. It gave me great comfort to know that there was a pony place waiting for me if I could reach it. Whenever I was sad or lonely, when life seemed very hard, I let my mind wander to that sunny slope of snow.

The men sold me to another man, a Russian, short and fat, who liked to spit a lot. The first thing he did when he saw me was hook his big fingers into my lips, pry them open, and peer at my teeth. His fingers tasted of horrible things, and his nails were like little stones jammed against my gums.

The Russian took me back to the forest. At first I thought it was kind of him to lead me there, and I hoped he would turn me loose to run again with the wild ponies. But he led me instead to a camp in the mountains, far from the place where I was born. He had a gang of men who were cutting trees and trimming them down to timbers. I had to drag the logs out of the forest, with one man pulling at my head while another whipped my flanks with a willow stick. All day I pulled in the harness, through mud and snow, in cold and heat, for so many months that I lost track of them all, and the months turned into years. In summer, flies laid eggs in the long welts across my back, and the itching nearly drove me mad. In winter, the maggots froze, bringing relief in one way but agony in another. With every smack of the stick, I screamed.

There was not even a stable. I was tied to a tether near the bunkhouse, where the men all slept. When the weather was cold, I shivered for hours, and when it was warm, the flies came so thickly that I thought I'd be eaten alive. Every night, I hoped that I would slip away in my sleep and find myself at the gateway. I dreamed of that, of galloping up the slope to the ponies' place.

The work lasted five years, and when it was done, so was I. Just eight years old, I felt like seventeen.

❄   ❄   ❄

On a day in early spring, with patches of snow still on the ground, I was led out of the forest for the last time. The Russian drove a wagon and pulled me behind it, down through the valley, along a skidding trail that met a road that led us to the east.

After several days of traveling, we came to a dry valley where a huge wall stretched clear across the land. It rose from the ridge to the south, dipped through the valley and up to the ridge to the north, like a stone snake curled across the hills. And in the middle of the valley was a city.

What a bustle of people there were! By the thousands they hurried in every direction, like ants on a great mound, churning a haze of dust. Street sellers called out to the Russian, trying to sell him rugs and shoes and animals of every kind, both alive and dead. Little black monkeys chattered in their cages as they reached pink hands through the bars. But the Russian never turned his head as he drove along, tugging me through the city.

In a dirty field below the wall, a horse fair was under way. A mob of ponies had been gathered on a bit of grass, and thousands of people had come to buy them. Some of the ponies were being ridden madly through the crowd while others stood in long, tethered rows. Many looked old and weary, but just as many were strong young things, with years of work ahead of them. A few were utterly mad, turning in fury on any man who came too close.

The Russian gave me up to a dirty little Mongol in black clothes, in exchange for a very small handful of money. He looked at me one last time, and spat at my feet.

I was glad to be rid of him but frightened as well, for it seemed that every change took me to something worse, that each of my owners was more horrid than the last. The Mongol grabbed my halter and hauled me off across the fairground. His hair, in a filthy pigtail, swung back and forth across his neck.

I expected to be put in among the other strong ponies, to be sent to work again in the forest. But instead, I joined a sad little group that no buyer was bothering to look at. I was tethered among the old and the sick, with those who were crazy and those who had never been tamed. I couldn't imagine that anyone would buy them, and I wondered—for the first time—what happened to worn-out ponies. Were they turned loose in the forest to find their old herds? Were they put out to pasture in a farmer's field, with nothing to do but sleep and eat? Or was there something else that I couldn't even imagine? I hoped for the best but feared for the worst.

⁂   *⁂*   *⁂*

All day we stood in the heat and the dust and the sun. People passed in great numbers, and the Mongol grew more and more fretful. He waved his arms faster; he shouted louder. He began to reach out and grab the sleeves of passing men.

Most shook him off with a disdainful look, as though the dirty little Mongol was another monkey in a cage. The only man who stopped to look at me was strangely pale and pink. He was an Englishman, the first I'd ever seen, with a Russian boy walking beside him.

The Englishman looked me over from head to toe. He came closer, lifting his arm toward me. I flinched. But instead of hitting me, the Englishman froze. He stood with his hand in the air until I stopped trembling. Then he looked me right in the eye.

"It's all right," he said softly. "I'm not going to hurt you. I promise."

I sensed a caring in his voice, a tone I'd never heard. He reached out again, this time very slowly, and I tried not to shake, in case that made him angry. I let him stroke my nose. I let him pat the place between my ears and comb his fingers through my forelock. At first I wanted to run away. But he said, "There, there," in that quiet voice, and I just closed my eyes and shivered.

The Mongol looked surprised. Then he grabbed the boy by the arm, and the two babbled madly in Russian. They waved their arms, they shouted, but the Englishman kept petting me. When he took his hand away, I was disappointed. I snorted and moved a bit closer, hoping he would touch me again. But now *he* was the one who shied away, and I saw that he was a little bit afraid of me, as I had been of him. He didn't feel safe with a big animal pressing against him. So he moved to my shoulder and rubbed the muscles there, and when he found the scars in my skin, he touched them very gently. His fingers lingered on the spot where a man had broken a bottle long ago. He said in a whisper, "Someone's done some very dreadful things to you."

The Mongol and the Russian were still talking, though now less frantically. The Englishman reached into his pocket, a quick movement that alarmed me. I skittered off with a frightened little whimper. For a moment he froze again. Then his hand slowed down, and when it came out of his pocket, I saw that he was holding a small white cube, like a tiny block of snow. He lifted it to my mouth, his hand splayed as flat as a stone.

I had lived eight years but never tasted sugar. I couldn't believe that anything could be so good. I hoped there was another block of sugar in the Englishman's pocket, so I nudged against him, and that made him laugh. "Ah," he said. "I've got a friend for life now, haven't I?" Then he rubbed my nose again and turned toward his companion. "What do you think of this one?" he asked.

"Good pony," said the boy. He gestured down the row of old animals as the Mongol smiled slyly behind him. "All ponies, good ponies."

The Englishman stroked his chin. I tried to follow him when he walked down the row, but only tugged up on my tether. I hoped he would buy me.

He looked only at the light-colored ponies. All others he

passed right by, though some were the best of all. When he was far down the line, I heard a pony nicker, and another cry out in fear. I saw one rear up, suddenly rising above the others. It snorted and whinnied; it struck out with its forelegs. Then the Englishman stumbled backward, and the boy tried to pull him away.

The pony kept rising up on its hind legs, plunging and rising again. Dimly at first, I remembered that pony. When I saw the dark patch on its chest, a thousand memories came back very clearly. It was the silvery stallion I had known long ago, the leader who had watched over me when I was young. He was more gray now than silver. His back was bent, his shoulders strained from pulling, and his eyes had a wild stare that made him seem quite mad. But as he towered up on his hind legs, mane and forelock flying, he looked just as strong and magnificent as ever.

I called out in a high-pitched whinny, but there was no answer from the stallion. I saw the Englishman get up and slap bits of straw from his clothes. "Well, that one's got spirit," he said.

He bought the stallion. He bought nineteen others, including me. Most were old or mean or angry, but all as white as snow. The Englishman seemed very pleased with himself, though the Mongol was even more delighted.

That very day—that very hour—we were led away by the Russian boy. Some, like the stallion, fought him all the way. They kicked and bucked so wildly that people ran to hide in doorways. But in the end, the boy won. He got us to the railway yard, and a train arrived in the morning.

The train had a whistle that was high and shrill, like the cry of a frightened rabbit. I looked toward the sound and saw smoke above the buildings, a line of gray and black. The huffs and puffs of the engine pulsed in the air like the breaths of a terrible creature. Then the engine came chugging around a corner, black and filthy, snorting steam, swaying from side to side.

It frightened me. I had never seen a train, and I didn't like the sounds or smells. When the smoke wafted over us, we all jostled uneasily, every pony trying to find a bit of space where there wasn't even room to turn around.

A Russian standing guard shouted at us to be quiet. He whacked the fence with his stick.

The engine's breaths grew louder. It whistled again with a piercing blast, and the stallion started kicking. He reared up and bashed at the fence, his ears pressed back, his nostrils flaring. He flung himself against the boards, wanting only to get away.

The man shouted again. He made his stick swish and whistle as he swung it at the stallion. He struck the pony across the eye, and a dark line opened in the silvery hair.

The stallion cowered back. He blinked and hung his head with a sad little whimper.

I had seen that pony drive away a mountain bear. I had watched him take on three wolves at once, kicking at two while he grabbed the third with his teeth. But now he was just an old and frightened thing, flinching from a willow branch.

The man stood up on the fence rails. He hit every pony that he could reach and didn't stop until he was out of breath. He was coughing then, doubled over with his hands on his knees, still holding the stick that dripped with our sweat and our blood.

❄   ❄   ❄

I hoped the train would take me to the ponies' place. In a sense it did, though the journey was so long and so hard that I couldn't have known it started then.

We were pushed aboard a cattle car, and a door was slammed behind us. It was dark in there, and scary, until the sun found his way between the boards. He reached through narrow cracks and knotholes, touching my ribs. A golden mist of trampled straw floated in the air, making me sneeze and snort. With a puff of the engine and a jolt of cars, we started on our way.

It was hard to balance against the rolling of the train. We all swayed and rocked together, like the fat women who danced in the lumber camps. Through day and night the train carried us on, stopping only when the engine was thirsty. I was thirsty too, but there was no water for me, though I heard it splashing out across the tracks at every watering place.

We traveled through forests that smelled of moss and mushrooms, reminding me of my first days. We crossed a range of stony hills, rattling over many bridges above rivers that roared and foamed. We went all the way to the ocean, and down to the docks where the Englishman was waiting.

His name, I learned, was Mr. Meares. He brought along a

18

doctor who looked us over and shook his head. The doctor told Mr. Meares that someone had pulled wool over his eyes, which seemed a strange thing to say. "They're the poorest lot of animals I've ever seen," he said. He pointed to a wheezy pony whose shoulders were crooked from pulling carts. "That one stays behind."

"Why?" asked the Englishman.

"Just look at him," said the doctor. "He's got glanders, for starters. He'll give it to the rest, and likely to you as well."

So the pony stayed behind. On a hot and rainy day, nineteen of us were loaded onto an old steamer that was stained with rust. One by one we were hoisted in a wooden box that swayed at the end of a rope.

I was scared to get into that box and swing up through the air. I didn't know where the ship would take me. I wanted to go back to the forests, even back to the lumber camps if I could. The stallion was more frightened than me. When the men came to take him, he bolted. He pulled away, smashed through the fence, and went galloping down the dock.

Another pony followed, the two of them racing through a crowd of people who scattered like locusts. But they were soon caught and dragged back, soon loaded on the ship.

It was my turn next, and I trembled in the box. I closed my eyes so I wouldn't see the water underneath me, and when the box thumped down on the deck, I thought the bottom had fallen open. I was taken out and put into a very narrow stall. It didn't seem so bad, really—until the dogs came aboard.

They were big and vicious things, with enormous teeth and narrow eyes. They seemed wild as wolves, or even wilder, and bared their teeth at men, at ponies, at each other. They were chained to railings and boxes and machines until the ship seemed covered with dogs. Every one of them howled and barked without stopping.

Like every pony, I feared dogs more than anything else. I didn't feel safe with them all around me, but all I could do was close my eyes and pretend they weren't there.

Then the ship headed out to sea, and I went toward a new life. I didn't expect anything but misery.

These things I'd learned when I was young: Life is short and men are cruel, and ponies are born to suffer. I decided that I would work as hard as I could at whatever job I was given, believing that I would earn my reward in the end and live forever in the ponies' place.

In the ponies' place, men would serve the animals. In the ponies' place, the stables would be warm, well padded with straw, and the blankets would come straight from the stove, still hot and soft and smoky-smelling. My scars would heal at the ponies' place. And not once in ten thousand years would I feel the sting of whip or lash.

.

In London, on the first of June, Captain Scott's ship leaves for the south. Her name is Terra Nova. She's an old Scottish whaler, built for the Arctic, armed against ice. She has three masts and a tall funnel that spews smoke among the sails. A steam engine deep in her hold burns three tons of coal every hour.

There's a crowd cheering on the dock as she sets out into the river. Tiny children wave good-bye to their fathers. Women weep and laugh at once. They all watch until the ship rounds the bend and passes out of sight. But they still hear the whistles of boats and barges and ships, every vessel on the river saluting the Terra Nova as she passes.

Scott is not aboard. Still short of money for his expedition, he stays behind to finish his preparations. Six weeks later, with his wife but not their newborn son, he takes the fast mail ship to Africa to meet the Terra Nova down in Capetown.

He knows that other men are hoping to reach the Pole. But he believes he's far ahead of anyone else. He plans to go slowly, giving his scientists time for their work.

In Capetown, he takes command of the Terra Nova and sets off for Australia. He finds that his old whaler leaks quite badly, and he's disappointed by her slow speed and great appetite for coal.

The voyage takes longer than he'd planned. He leaves the ship and sends her on to New Zealand, where his ponies and dogs are already waiting. On shore in Melbourne, he finds old mail that's been kept for his arrival. Among the many letters is a telegram.

It's a very short message from Amundsen:

BEG LEAVE INFORM YOU
PROCEEDING ANTARCTIC

The telegram is dated September 9, 1910. It was sent from Spain and is already five weeks old.

Scott hurries off again, making his way to New Zealand to join his ship and push on to the Pole.

Chapter Two

THE voyage on the old steamer was a misery, for the most part. I was not used to a floor that moved underneath me, and the roll of the ship made me terribly sick. The sun was too hot, the sea too bright. The stench from the dogs was unbearable.

I wanted water all the time but got it only twice a day, when the Russian boy came around with a bucket. I always leaned toward it over the top of my stall, my lips fluttering at the lovely smell of water. But every time, just as I started to drink, the Russian whipped away the bucket.

My legs ached because I couldn't lie down. My back itched from the soot that fell from the funnel, a black rain that covered almost everything except the wretched dogs. They watched me endlessly, their savage little eyes just slits in their fur.

Sometimes Mr. Meares came by and petted me, but not very often. He cared more about the dogs than he did about the ponies. It was the same with his dog driver, a Russian I seldom saw and never grew to like. And the boy—a jockey—was so excited by the journey that he sometimes forgot about the ponies.

We sailed south forever, right through the winter without even seeing it. We left in summer and finished in spring, with a fiery sun growing hotter every day.

We landed on an island where the grass grew green and thick, where the trees were wide and shady. There was a sandy beach to run along, and we raced through the shallows, kicking up foam.

This wasn't at all what I'd expected. Some of the ponies, especially the older ones, would have lived happily there forever. The heat was good for their bones, while the sun made them sleepy and lazy, and there were often three or four sprawled on the grass at once. I had to stand in the shade, swatting insects with my tail. I was a winter pony, with a thick mane and shaggy hair. I liked crisp mornings when I breathed white steam, rivers of ice-cold water, and mountains with snow on their tops.

But for the moment, I was very happy. The whip and the lash were as scarce as icicles. The men seemed to have no meanness in them. Yet I couldn't believe I would never be hit, and so I flinched whenever a man raised a hand to scratch his hair or trim his hat. "Easy, lad," I heard a hundred times a day. "Easy, lad. I'm not going to hurt you."

Mr. Meares put on short trousers and soon turned his legs to the same fiery shade as his face. He grew enormous stains of sweat on the back and the arms of his shirt, and he wore a handkerchief underneath his hat to shield himself twice from the sun.

It was a disappointment to some of the ponies when he brought out harnesses and traces. But I liked to work, so I didn't mind, though I couldn't understand our job. We dragged logs up and down the beach, logs so heavy that they didn't even float. We pulled them to the end of the beach, then turned around and pulled them back. There was no sense to the work, but we learned the English way to pull and haul. It was a gentler way, with a guiding hand on the halter and a biscuit when we finished. I was soon throwing myself gladly at the harness, eager to please Mr. Meares.

I wished that the stallion and some of the others would settle down and lose their fears. To them, every man in the world was a fearsome figure.

One day a gentleman came wandering down from his house, white haired and stiff backed, with a lady clinging to his arm. He stopped to admire the stallion, and asked the jockey, "How old is that one there?" The jockey only shrugged; he didn't know. So the gentleman went closer to have a look.

The stallion tried to warn the man away. He pinned his ears back; he put his head low to the ground and swung it back and forth. But the man didn't notice—or didn't understand—and only went closer. So the stallion charged him.

The old man just stood there, maybe too surprised to run. In an instant, the stallion was right in front of him, rearing up to strike him down.

At the last moment, the gentleman raised one skinny little arm, trying to ward off the pony with his walking stick. Then the stallion struck out and the man went flying backward onto the grass. With a shriek, the stallion reared again and plunged with his hooves.

It took four big men to pull the pony away. He bucked and kicked and struggled. The men were scared, but awed as well. He was such a vicious fighter that he earned the name Hackenschmidt, after the famous Russian wrestler who had never lost a fight.

I saw his eyes that day, all wild and crazy, and I wondered again what had happened to him in his life among men. He was so angry, so bitter, that he frightened other ponies. There was just one with no fear of him—another stallion a little younger, every bit as wild himself. The men called that one Christopher, which I thought was too nice a name for such a horrible pony.

They were like a pair of bullies, Hackenschmidt and Christopher, staying friends only to keep themselves from killing each other. Both were stubborn and still untamed. As soon as the halters and traces were brought out, the two ponies made it clear they didn't want to work. But the men were even more stubborn, and though it sometimes took four or five of them to do it, they always got those ponies harnessed. They always got them working, and they did it without a stick or whip.

I decided that they were training us for a special task, because no men—not even Englishmen—worked just for the pleasure of working. I wondered endlessly what it might be, and watched for clues in everything.

The first hint came in November, when a strange ship arrived at our island. It was Captain Scott's *Terra Nova*, but I didn't know it then. All I noticed was a funnel that spewed black smoke, and an old smell of death covered over with paint and tar.

※　　※　　※

The ship was still moving along the jetty when men began to come ashore. They were like fleas leaping from a dog, bounding from the side of it.

One of those men had a pipe in his teeth. He walked for a while in a funny way, as if the land was moving underneath him, though it wasn't. He went up and down the jetty, then turned and came straight for the ponies.

He walked quickly, in long strides. He marched across the ground to the field where we were grazing, and he put his elbows on the fence and leaned there, puffing his pipe.

Hackenschmidt and Christopher snorted anxiously. They cantered away to the far side of the field, and some of the other ponies followed. But I stood where I was, not three yards away from the man. I liked him right away, because he smiled when he looked at me.

Over his shoulder, I could see Mr. Meares walking toward us, his pink legs flashing in the sunlight. He called out, "What do you think of them, Titus?"

The new man took the pipe from his mouth. He talked loudly, without turning his head. "They look first class."

He had the kindliest voice I'd ever heard, and a feeling of compassion that hovered around him like his pipe smoke. I wanted to greet him properly, with a good sniff and a rub, but I went cautiously, with my head down and my hooves scuffing through the grass. I snorted softly to show him I wouldn't be any trouble.

He didn't move a muscle. He kept leaning on the fence, now holding the pipe in his hand, watching me with bright, sea-colored eyes.

I stopped in front of him, near enough that he could touch me if he wanted to. For a long time we looked at each other. Then he suddenly leaned forward.

He was quick as a snake. Before I knew it, he had grabbed hold of my halter. I tried to pull away.

"Easy, lad," he said, seeing how I shivered. "You're safe as houses, son."

I moved closer. I nudged against him, and he smiled again at that. Then his eyes shifted away, and he looked at the scars on my shoulders. He touched them, and I didn't even flinch.

This man was Lawrence Oates, a soldier, a captain in the cavalry. No one ever called him by his real name. To the men, he was Titus or the Soldier. But to me he seemed so much unlike a fighting man that he was only *Mister* Oates.

He didn't stay long that day. After a little pet and a rub on the cheek, he went away with Mr. Meares, strolling together toward the ship. From then on, I watched for him all the time, standing whenever I could at the same spot along the fence. But it was three or four days before I saw him coming toward me again.

It took me by surprise. I was watching for him around the ship, but he appeared instead on the roadway, in a happy group of people.

It was a fine day, the clouds like froth on a river. Honey-bees were buzzing around the clovers, and the people came slowly in the sunshine, chattering away like crows.

In the middle of the group was a man with a walking stick, wearing a cap with a gleaming badge, and a coat with rows of buttons that flashed in the sun in rounds of gold. The others swarmed around him—now in front, now behind—like a flock of little birds. He had Mr. Oates close behind him, and a woman at his side, the most beautiful creature I had ever seen. Her white clothes reached right to the ground, and I had to wonder if she had any legs, because she seemed to float like a cloud across the grass. At the back of the group, the Russian jockey carried lead ropes draped across his shoulders.

The man in the middle was Captain Scott. He swung his walking stick in his hand, jaunty as a wooden tail. Ten yards away, he stopped and stared at me and the other ponies. He pushed up the brim of his cap.

The whole group stopped along with him. Mr. Meares came up to his side, beaming proudly. Mr. Oates lingered, though I longed for him to come up and pet me.

Captain Scott studied us carefully. For once, all of us were quiet, no one fighting another. Even Hackenschmidt was doing nothing more than eating grass, though he was wary as he did it. We must have made a splendid sight: nineteen white ponies in a field of grass and clover.

"Splendid," said Captain Scott. He looked very pleased. "A bit of all right. Don't you agree, Titus?"

"They seem so," said Mr. Oates. "I haven't had a proper look yet."

"No time like the present," said Captain Scott.

The whole group came through the gate and into the field. The Russian jockey ran ahead and gathered four ponies, including me. He attached our lead ropes and held us in a bunch as Captain Scott and the others came toward us. The lady kept her distance, making sure there was a man between herself and any pony. But Mr. Meares and Captain Scott came right among us, and then Mr. Oates—with his pipe in his teeth— smiled right at me. "There's my lad," he said.

I was thrilled that Mr. Oates remembered me. I greeted him with a snort and a nicker and a toss of my head. It made the men laugh for some reason, and the lady cried out, "What a darling!"

I was the first to be examined. Captain Scott held my rope while Mr. Oates looked me over. He lifted my feet and poked my hooves; he felt my belly and my chest. He wasn't smiling anymore; he was frowning instead. He moved on to the next pony, and the next after that, until he'd looked at all four of us.

Captain Scott seemed impatient. "Well?" he said.

"They've had a hard life," said Mr. Oates with a sigh. "A long one too."

"Do you mean they're old?" asked the captain.

"As the hills," said Mr. Oates. "They're worn out. A lot of crocks, most of them."

Crocks. It was the first time I'd heard that word. But I could tell it wasn't a good thing to be a crock. The ponies beside me *were* old; it was true. Their coats were ragged, their backs bent, their teeth badly worn. I wondered if Hackenschmidt was a crock because he was so wild. Or Christopher because he was stubborn and mean.

Mr. Meares looked disappointed. And Captain Scott

seemed almost angry. "You're being a bit hard on them, don't you think?" he said.

Mr. Oates shook his head. "Not at all."

"Well, I believe they'll do very well," said Captain Scott. "They're as good as Shackleton's; I'm sure of that."

There was another new word. I was glad to be better than a shackleton, though I had no idea what it was.

"They'll do the job," said Captain Scott.

The job. I pricked up my ears, hoping to learn something more. But the captain walked away with Mr. Oates and all the rest. So I began to stand around the edges of the field, trying to hear important words. Everything was a puzzle.

When the men began to empty the ship, I hoped they were staying on the island. The things they unloaded were made for cold weather: big sledges and tents and woolly clothes. But they only emptied the ship to make repairs, and then they filled it again. The work took many days, and I spent most of them lying on the grass, eating every tiny clover I could reach without moving. Each morning, the lady brought a parasol and sat beside me, scratching my ears as I nibbled away.

But the work came to an end eventually, and one evening, all of the men got onto the ship.

I was afraid they were leaving without me. I called out to Mr. Oates. I whinnied and nickered for all I was worth. But he didn't notice. So I dashed back and forth along the fence, crying out like a colt for its mother. But for once—for the first time—Mr. Oates did not come to see me.

❄ ❄ ❄

In the morning, everything seemed a disaster. The jetty was empty, the ship was loaded, and black smoke billowed from the funnel. I felt a terrible lurch inside my chest. It would be hard enough to watch him sail away, but even worse if Mr. Oates didn't come and say good-bye.

But the ship didn't leave. Instead, a huge box appeared, rising from the muddled deck. It made bad memories in my mind, but I didn't run away. I moved closer instead, hoping to be first aboard.

The men took Hackenschmidt. Six of them wrestled him into the box, and he kicked and bucked all the time. It was the same for Christopher, and I was next after him. A big sailor named Taff Evans gave me a biscuit as he guided me into the box. "That's the ticket," he said proudly. "That's how it's done."

He rubbed my ears, then closed the box, and up I went. The men laughed to see me looking down at them as I munched away on my biscuit.

Mr. Oates was waiting on the ship. "There's my lad," he said as he let me out of the box. "Midships," he told a sailor, who led me to my place, down a deck so crowded with crates and sacks that we had to go in single file. I was given a stall in a row of four, with a roof of canvas cloth. I could look up toward the bow, or over the roof of the icehouse, past the funnel toward the stern. I had to peer between packing crates and machinery, but it was a pleasant view. Other ponies, not as lucky, were put right into the ship, in a dark space below the deck.

When the last pony was aboard, the dogs came barking across the island. I had thought I was rid of them, but again they were chained all around me. One was tied right in front of my stall, another only a few feet away, a few on the roof of the icehouse. I hoped their chains were good and strong, and I wished they'd stop their howling.

The steam engine started thumping below me. Puffs of smoke rose from the funnel like black thunderheads. With a shrill from the whistle, and a cheer from the shore, we started on our way. Captain Scott shouted orders, the men hauled on the ropes, and the ship moved faster every moment. The thumping of the engine made everything shake and rattle and jingle. I saw the captain wave at his wife, who had stayed on the shore, then turn his back toward her. Soon we left the shelter of the land and came out to the open sea.

❄ ❄ ❄

Despite the never-ending roll of the ship, and the dogs at my feet, I found the early days of that voyage were some of the happiest of my life.

Of the nineteen ponies, I was the sailors' favorite. They named me James Pigg, in honor of a man who lived only in a book. "A pleasant rogue," they said. Sometimes they called me Jimmy Pigg, and sometimes only James. And they always said it in the fondest way, with a smile and a thump on my shoulder. Often, there was a biscuit as well, slipped to me from a cupped hand so the other ponies wouldn't be jealous. "You're a good lad, James Pigg," they said.

It was the first time in my life that I had a name. In the past, I had always been "the pony," just a *thing* that pulled a cart or dragged a log. But now I felt important.

We all got names. A lazy old pony on my left became Weary Willy. A small one on my right was named Jehu, the one beside him, Nobby. I heard other names shouted through the wall, from the space where the ponies were stabled. I never saw the ponies in there but learned of Snatcher and Snippets, and Bones and Guts, and so many others that I couldn't keep track.

I sometimes heard the sailors singing, and the ship felt safe and happy. But as we went along to the south, the wind blew harder. The sea grew very rough. I saw the men turn anxious faces toward the sky as it filled with wicked clouds.

There was a terrible storm. It began with wind that howled like a dog. Then the waves got bigger and bigger, and soon the ship was rolling heavily. I had to struggle to stay on my feet as I was driven back and forth against the ends of my stall.

The ship rolled so far that I thought it would roll right over. Waves came thundering over the side, surging across the deck. They leapt over the icehouse and burst against my stall. I was suddenly belly deep in water, and it slowly drained away.

For the dogs it was worse. Buried by every wave, they struggled at the ends of their chains. They didn't bark anymore; they didn't howl. They whimpered like baby birds, looking around with fear-filled eyes. Even I felt sorry for them.

The wind grew stronger. The waves grew higher. Packing crates and bags of coal shifted back and forth, battering at the railing and the deckhouse.

Then a chunk of railing broke away. It tumbled into the

sea, and a struggling dog, chained to the wood, paddled furiously for a moment before he was dragged under. He rose again, swimming for all he was worth, then disappeared forever.

I believed the ship was drowning. It wallowed in the waves like a great hog in a slough of mud. I could smell fear in the men, but they kept at work. Only a few were sailors. Most were scientists and doctors. There was a cook, and a photographer who'd been seasick on the calmest days. But every man turned out to save the ship, and they did it. They pitched coal over the side by the ton. They pumped water from the hull and lifted it up by the bucket.

A rainbow appeared as they worked. It was the most beautiful rainbow I'd ever seen, huge and bright across the sky. One man saw it and nudged his neighbor, and soon every one of them was looking toward that rainbow. Then the next huge wave collapsed on the deck, and the work began again.

I lost my balance as the ship pitched sideways. My front legs slithered out from under me, and down I went, crashing forward into the boards. I couldn't get up and couldn't lie down, and I thought my legs were about to snap. I heard a wave thundering over the ship, and my stall suddenly filled with water.

I panicked. I kicked and thrashed on the floor of my stall; I screamed from fear and pain. The sea roared in, covering me again, and little Jehu had to scamper and jump to keep away from my flailing hooves.

It was a sailor who saw me, a man called Thomas Crean. He shouted for help, and Mr. Oates came running. "Hang on, lad," he said as he clambered into the stall.

Just the sound of his voice was calming. I lay heaving on the floor as he untangled my legs. The big round face of Taff Evans peered down at me over the boards. Then he joined Mr. Oates in my stall, and the two of them hauled me to my feet just as my mother had done on the day I was born. They held me up till I found my balance. They braced me against the side.

"There you go, Jimmy," said Taff Evans. "Up on your pegs, eh. Bob's your uncle."

When he saw that I was safe, Mr. Oates hurried away. I could hear the ponies struggling in the dark space inside the ship, screaming as they bashed against the wood.

At the stern stood Captain Scott, as ragged as a scarecrow. He steered to the east with the wind behind him. To me, the ship seemed frightened. It ran at a crazy speed, hurtling through the waves. Captain Scott didn't seem worried. But I thought the ship had bolted and was running just for the sake of running.

The Terra Nova *is sinking. Captain Scott keeps her running east, hoping the storm will pass. He relies on the steam engine to pump water from the hull of the old whaler.*

Down below, everything is wet. Seawater drips through the coal bunkers, washing the dust down to the bilge. In the bottom of the ship, it sloshes back and forth, mixing with lubricating oil spilled from the engine. Bit by bit it's drawn into the pumps, where it turns to a black and tarry mass. It clogs the valves; it chokes the pumps.

In the engine room, water rises quickly over the gratings. The engine is shut down to save the boilers.

The Terra Nova is heavy in the water now, and the waves roll right over the deck. Captain Scott, standing at the stern, can see nothing of his ship but the masts. Two ponies are battered to death in their stalls. A dog is carried overboard. Ten tons of coal are lost, along with sixty-five gallons of gasoline meant to power the motor sledges.

Scott puts his scientists to work with buckets, lifting water from the bilge. His sailors chop though a bulkhead to reach the clogged pumps.

Scientists with buckets, and sailors with axes, manage to save the old ship. The storm passes and Scott turns south again.

❄ ❄ ❄

Amundsen and his Fram are far to the west, trailing Scott by thousands of miles. He has just passed the Kerguelen Islands, halfway between Africa and Australia. He had hoped to visit the Norwegian whaling station there, but bad weather kept him at sea. Now the winds are fair, and he's bowling along toward Antarctica. He has four thousand miles to go.

His ship is covered with dogs. He left Norway with ninety-seven, but puppies have been born at sea, and there are now considerably more. They run loose, not minding the gales but hating the rain.

CHAPTER THREE

I didn't know that two ponies had died until I saw their bodies being hoisted through the skylight.

It was awful to see them so slack and limp, as lifeless as the bags of coal. A group of sailors dragged the bodies across the deck, waited until the ship rolled heavily, then heaved them over the rail. Poor Mr. Oates looked brokenhearted.

I saw him leaning against the rigging, staring into the sea, and I wished I could go and prop him up, as he had held me through the storm. I knew what he was thinking, that it had not been fair to the ponies to drag them half a world away from forest and field, to see them die in a ship on the ocean. I imagined that he was afraid the ponies hated him for it.

All the men stopped work for a moment as the dead ponies

plunged into the sea. Spray flew up and splattered on Mr. Oates's boots. He looked horrified by that. Then the sailors went back to work, but Mr. Oates stayed where he was. He got out his pipe and lit it, and turned up his face to the sky.

Compared to me, he was small and frail. But at that instant, he seemed as strong as an ox, and I knew I would follow him to the end of the earth if that was where he cared to lead me.

❄ ❄ ❄

South, south, forever to the south, the ship moved along over rounded waves, to wherever it was we were going.

We saw the first iceberg of the voyage. It was far to the west, hard for me to see at all. The men were all excited, shouting at each other to look. I leaned to the right and peered between two rows of packing crates. I saw the iceberg far away as sunlight glowed on its top. It looked to me like a lump of sugar, glistening on a gray plate of sea and sky.

On that same day, we saw sleek fish that the men called dolphins, a very playful sort of fish. The men gathered in the bow to watch them roll and spin. It gave me a small pang to see Mr. Oates among them, smiling so broadly that I wondered if he preferred fish over ponies.

The dogs, of course, went into a barking frenzy at the puffing sound of dolphin breaths. They did the same with the birds and the chunks of ice that began to appear in the following days. Soon, there was ice all around us, and birds all above us, and the dogs were seldom silent. The photographer, a man named Mr. Ponting, took pictures of everything that moved and many things that didn't.

Then the ice grew thicker, and soon the ship could go no farther. We sat in a field of white slabs that stretched forever in all directions. The sails furled, the engine stilled; we just floated there, waiting for a channel to appear.

We waited for hours. We waited for days. The men grew bored with all the waiting and just stood along the rails and up on the mast, for once as mindless as the dogs. They pointed out everything that moved, from the great whales spouting among the floes, to the tiniest of birds. They shouted at some of the things. They shot at others, the hollow bark of their guns a flat sound with no echo. But mostly they laughed, and they laughed particularly loudly at the fat little birds they called penguins, the sorriest sort of bird I'd ever seen.

Standing upright on flat feet, with little round bellies and stubby wings, the penguins came waddling toward us in huge numbers. All black and white, like little men in little suits, they swayed from side to side. They sometimes toppled over. Far in the distance, I could see more coming, and more behind those, and distant dark specks, all moving in columns and rows.

Now and then the ice parted with a shudder, and the ship moved along again, sometimes under sail and sometimes with the engine. Some days we gained less than a mile, and on others we slipped backward, carried along in the floes. Once in a while we came to a bit of open water and sailed a long way, only to jam up in the ice again and begin our waiting all over.

All the days were the same, except for one called Christmas. On that day, Mr. Oates brought me a special sort of biscuit. Then Taff Evans brought an oil cake, and I could hardly believe my luck to get two fine treats in one day, for doing nothing but standing in my stall. But Christmas wasn't even finished yet. Captain Scott came by after dinner, and three or four others after him, all arriving one by one. I got more treats and pets that day than I'd had in my whole life before it.

The last to come was a sailor named Patrick Keohane, who had a funny way of talking because he lived in a place called Ireland. He gave me a piece of apple, the first I'd had in a very long time. Then he stood for a while and petted me. "Do you know they'll all be in church in Ireland just now?" he said. "Yes, sitting in church, and probably saying a prayer for me too. All day I've been thinking of them. Oh, I was missing my home this morning." The sailor's hands were tough and red. He squeezed my ear in his fist, in a way that was firm and gentle at the same time. "I was thinking of the sheep. Of the shamrocks," he said. "Everything's green in Ireland, all the year round. You'd fancy that, wouldn't you?"

I nodded my head. I snorted softly as I pressed against him. He stroked the side of my nose.

"You poor thing; you've no idea what you're in for." He chuckled quietly. "I'm not even sure that I know it myself. But I've got a sense of what's coming, and you don't, and I wonder: Who's the lucky one, then? Oh, I'd change places with you quick enough, I think."

He might have stayed and talked to me for a long time. But another sailor came by, and Mr. Keohane suddenly seemed a bit embarrassed to be talking to a pony. He gave me a friendly cuff, then moved slowly away.

"Merry Christmas to you, James Pigg," he said.

The sun swung very low in the north. The ice turned to many colors, to many shades of blue and red. Then down in the ship, the men started singing. Their songs were solemn and slow, but I felt happy that night, like a shipmate of them all.

❄   ❄   ❄

On the last day of the year, Captain Scott saw the mountains on the land ahead. He was standing at the rail with his head poking over a packing crate, staring eagerly to the south like a groundhog poking its head from a hole.

When he saw the mountains, he cheered. Then everyone looked, and everyone cheered, and I could feel an excitement sweep over the ship like a fire. Even the dogs stirred restlessly, sensing that something had changed, or that something was about to happen. Captain Scott wore an expression of triumph, as though his goal had been only to *see* the mountains, that he could now turn the ship around and head for home.

But the ship pressed on. The ice ground against the hull, forced aside as we moved south toward those mountains. And two hours later, though it didn't matter to me, one year ended and another began.

In the counting of men, it was now 1911.

On the third day of the year, we saw the land along the sea. What a terrible place we'd come to, a world that seemed to guard itself with giant walls of ice and rock. There were mountains like dogs' teeth, and one with a plume of smoke streaming from a rounded top, as though a great fire burned inside it. Glaciers tumbled down between the peaks and calved into the sea with a constant roar and thunder. The cliff at the face of the glaciers was higher than the masts of the ship, and blocks of ice as big as houses split away and tumbled into the water. The sea churned at the foot of it, where icebergs rolled and tilted.

I felt a sense of dread as I peered out from my stall. I saw the faces of the men, suddenly grim and thoughtful. Through squinted eyes they looked at the snow and the ice, at the mountains, but not at each other. The land was so cold and barren that it made me shiver. I saw no trees, no flowers, no grass or clover, no plants of any sort.

But Captain Scott seemed perfectly happy. I could tell he was in love with this place. He had names for the mountains, for the bays and the capes, for the smoking peak with its white plume. He guided the ship along the edge of the ice cliff, around a point and around another. It was an island that we'd come to, but very different from the one we'd left. On three sides it was surrounded by ice, not water, and the only sand was in a black strip where I didn't feel like running at all.

Captain Scott knew every inch of it. A snow-covered beach appeared just where he said he would find one, and he brought the ship to the band of ice that floated in front of it, half a mile wide. The men set out anchors and moored to the ice. Their ropes froze stiff and straight, like iron rods.

Off went the dogs, led over the side. Then out came the pony box, and this time I was glad to see it. Weary Willy went first. He bounded from the box as soon as it was opened, threw himself down on the snow-covered ice and squirmed like a cat, flat on his back with his legs in the air. I was so excited that I could hardly stand still in the box. Like Weary Willy, the first thing I did was lie down and roll onto my back. Some of the men laughed at me. But I didn't care. It felt wonderful to stretch and scratch, to rub away the lice and the loose hair. My legs were happy because it was the first time in forty days that they didn't have to hold me up.

Weary Willy nibbled at my scabs and louse bites. I did the same for him, and then for Jehu and Nobby when they joined us. We stood in a happy group, all tending to one another.

There was a very nice man with a very big name. Mr. Apsley Cherry-Garrard. To me, and to everyone, he was only Cherry. He was twenty-six, which seemed ancient to a pony but not many years to a man. He looked after Weary Willy, and did it with nothing but kindness. Cherry could see only by peering through bits of glass hooked to his nose, as though he wore his eyes outside his head. It was his job to study the animals that lived in this winter land, and he was probably the happiest man on the whole ship because he was surrounded by the strangest animals.

There were fat seals sprawled on the ice like huge slugs. There were black skua birds that sat hunched in huge flocks and seemed like very evil little creatures. And there were penguins by the hundred, and they found Cherry just as interesting as he found them.

Penguins were curious about everything. They came from all around to have a look at us, waddling over the snow and the ice or popping up from the sea like sparks blown from a fire. They shot straight up at the edge of the ice, plopped flat on their bellies, then pushed themselves upright with their little stubs of wings. It amused me to see them.

In groups of five or six, they stood and stared at us. Their little heads twisted and bobbed, and they muttered to each other in soft twitters that were quite lovely to hear. When they tired of us, they moved on to the dogs and didn't know enough to be afraid. The dogs snarled and barked, but the penguins kept going closer. Mr. Meares shooed them away. He sent them scattering in their funny tilting steps, but they went right back as soon as they could. For a while, we watched a silly battle, with Mr. Meares running them off, and the penguins waddling back. But it wasn't long before one of them went too close.

It was the dog Osmon, the king of the dogs, who lured the bird toward him. He held back, letting the penguin think he was right at the end of his leash. He waited for his chance, then suddenly pounced. There was a wolfish snarl, a flash of teeth, the saddest little squeak from the penguin. Then its body lay torn on a stain of red snow, its feathers scattered across the ice. I shuddered inside, knowing the same thing could happen to me if Mr. Meares ever let his dogs get loose.

Even then, the penguins learned no lesson. I might have thought they had no fear at all, except they lived in dread of the killer whales.

They were the worst of all animals, the killer whales. They were black and white with piggish eyes and rows of teeth. They had tall fins on their backs that sliced through the water, and they came sometimes alone and sometimes in wolflike packs. They could swim at the speed of galloping horses, or float absolutely still with their heads high above the water. It was eerie to see them doing that, for they never made a sound while they floated there but just watched with their round eyes. Then down they went without a ripple, slipping quietly into the cold sea.

When the whales came close, I could hear their voices trembling through the ice. It was a faint sound of whistles and creaks, and at the first sound of it, the penguins burst from the water. Twenty, thirty, forty at once, the fat little birds exploded from the sea like rockets. And behind them, in the eddies and whirls of water, appeared scraps of penguin flesh.

Then the birds descended. Great flocks of black-winged skuas, all shrieking away, they came to feed on the scraps. I could follow the path of the orcas by the rising and falling of the birds.

It seemed a cruel world, really, in the icy land of the south. Seals hunted fish, and whales hunted seals, and everything hunted the poor penguins. The little babies tried their best to stay among the adults. But at least once in every hour a skua screamed and swooped, and a mother penguin was left bleating on the ice, gazing sadly all around.

I was glad there was nothing in that land to eat a pony, except the dreadful dogs.

For three days we did no work. Tied to a picket line on a snowy slope above the beach, we watched the men unload their things from ship to ice.

Off came the big packing crates that had covered so much of the deck. Inside them were strange sledges with motors on their backs. Instead of runners, they had wide belts that rolled round and round as the motors roared and clattered. They lurched along the ice, reeling over every hummock, while a gang of men scurried around to keep them moving straight and upright.

I was pleased when one of the sledges crashed through the ice and disappeared. But Captain Scott was so sad that I felt rotten for being happy. The other two motors went straight to work carrying loads of wood and canvas. Weary Willy loved to watch the machine doing his job, and the only thing that could have pleased him more would have been for the sledge to carry *him*.

Then out came harnesses for ponies and dogs, and another sort that I didn't understand. The men laid them out, attached the traces, then stepped right into those harnesses themselves. I could hardly believe it: men in harness, pulling like mad, puffing and grunting as ponies lounged nearby. I wondered if the cold and loneliness had driven them crazy. They even strapped boards to their feet—they called them "skis"—and went sliding across the ice, dragging a sledge piled high with bales of fodder.

It was a strange thing to stand idly, watching men work. In Russia, it would have pleased me; why, it would have *stunned* me. But now I felt useless, afraid that Captain Scott didn't believe ponies could work. I felt out of place; I wanted to do my share. To make things worse, the dogs were put in harness as well. They went dashing across the ice, pulling little sledges that were quick as lightning. A whole team pulled only three hundred pounds, a third of what I could manage on my own. Mr. Meares drove from the back of the sledges, shouting commands in Russian. *"Ki!"* he cried, and the dogs swung to the right. *"Tchui!"* he shouted, and they wheeled in a line to the left. With howls and barks, they made almost as much noise as the motor sledges.

I watched load after load come ashore. The men set up a winter station, starting with a big tent, and then a hut they built beside it. I thought I might never have a job to do.

At last I heard the jingle of a pony harness. To me, it was a lovely sound, but the work turned out to be harder than I'd thought it would be. There were so many supplies! We had to bring enough food and gear to see all of us through the winter, men and ponies and dogs. I found that dragging a sledge was not the same as dragging iron rails or heavy logs. If I slowed down, the sledge sometimes overtook me, and the heavy cross-bar banged against my legs. But if I tried to hurry, it stuck in soft snow and I jolted up against the traces. Still, I pulled nearly eight hundred pounds at a time, across the ice to the beach, up a hill to the building site. Then I trotted back for another load.

We all joined in, going round and round like the tracks on the motor sledges. I liked to see the long line of ponies, the leaders changing all the time. Uncle Bill, the biggest pony of all, pulled a thousand pounds on his sledge. But it was Michael, the smallest, who somehow pulled the fastest.

I was often overtaken. It seemed a long haul to me, from the ship to the hut, over the ice and up a slope. I didn't like that part of the work very much. I liked the parts better where I went back with the empty sledge, and where I waited while the men filled it again. A nice little man named Birdie Bowers was in charge of the stores, and he counted every bag and box like a chicken counting her eggs. He made sure that my sledge was never overfilled. Then Patrick Keohane, the Irishman, led me off again, and he let me amble along as I pleased.

Stubborn old Weary Willy went past me. So did Nobby, who was about my size, and even little Michael. But I overtook Blossom and Blucher, who were very old. And I fairly rocketed past poor ancient Jehu, who couldn't have passed a snail. The voyage had been hard on the oldest ponies, and he and Blossom and Blucher labored across the ice with their heads down, as though they were marching into a blizzard. Jehu's load was barely three hundred pounds, but he still wheezed with every step.

I slowed when I passed him for the first time. Our feet crunched together in the snow; the runners on our sledges rasped behind us. Jehu turned his head just enough to see that it was me, and his look was full of anguish. We knew what happened to ponies who couldn't keep up.

Then I saw his handler trudging along at his side. It was Mr. Atkinson, one of the doctors, and he looked just as worried as the pony.

"Poor old thing," he said. "Crocked out already. He won't last the summer. There's not a hope."

Mr. Keohane kept his hand in my halter. It was always there. I liked the feel of his knuckles pressing against my cheek, through the fur and hide of his mitten. We soon left Jehu behind.

Mr. Atkinson called out. "He'll be next, won't he? That one of yours."

"No, not James Pigg. Hardly," said Mr. Keohane. He tightened his hand on my halter, and I felt the press of his knuckles more tightly. "Don't you worry, lad," he said in his soft voice. "Don't you worry."

I didn't care very much just then for Mr. Atkinson. But I started wondering as I heaved my sledge along: Was I really a crock, no better than Jehu? Of course I wasn't a match for Uncle Bill. I wasn't as strong as Bones or Guts or Punch or Nobby. I couldn't go as steadily as Snatcher, or as quickly as Victor. But I hated to think that I was a crock.

I kicked the snow; I snorted. I decided right then to work harder, to work as hard as I possibly could. I would show Mr. Atkinson that he was wrong.

As I waited at the ship one day, Mr. Keohane left me to help Mr. Oates with Christopher. I stood a few yards from the edge of the ice, near the big anchor line that held the ship in place. Two of the dogs were tied to the rope, curled up like big furry balls.

Beyond them, in the water, the fins of killer whales appeared. I heard the puffs of the whales' breaths and saw the little clouds of spray. The dogs woke up, yawned and stretched. They looked at me hungrily.

The fins sliced quickly through the sea, rising and falling. Then they disappeared, all at once, and there was just the empty water.

But soon their heads appeared. They popped up together, a row of seven—young and old—staring toward me in that eerie way of theirs.

Captain Scott shouted from the ship. "Ponting! Look at the whales."

Mr. Ponting was taking pictures of penguins. He snatched up his big wooden camera and came running across the ice. He wore his coat and furry boots, a felt hat that bounced on his head.

The whales kept staring. Their teeth glistened in white rows. Mr. Ponting ran right up beside the dogs and knelt with his camera.

Suddenly, the whales disappeared. They sank into the water, all as one, and Mr. Ponting looked very disappointed. For a moment, nothing happened. Then the dogs started barking. They leapt at their tethers as though they were trying to jump right into the sea.

I felt a shudder in the ice. I felt another—a tremor that shook the floe. Mr. Ponting looked down at his feet, and I saw the ice bulge up around him. The dogs barked louder than ever. There was a big thud from below, a cracking of ice, and up came the back of a killer whale.

It pushed right through the floe, through twenty-four inches of ice. Mr. Ponting fell backward. With another thud and a boom, great cracks appeared in the ice, a spidery web that spread out in all directions. One raced toward me, zigzagging as it widened, and veered away just as it reached my hooves. A second whale burst through the floe, and a third behind him, and the booming went on and on underneath me.

The dogs' barking turned to howls and whines. Mr. Ponting leapt to his feet and sprinted across the ice as the cracks opened around him. He leapt from floe to floe. They tilted crazily, then flew apart, and up came a whale's head right behind Mr. Ponting. Its little round eye swiveled, seeking out the man. Its jaws opened and snapped shut, and Mr. Ponting raced for his life.

On every side of me, the ice cracked and split. The dogs whined; they shrieked. Mr. Meares ran flat out toward them, shouting at the whales. Mr. Keohane hurried to help me.

A strip of water appeared right at my feet, wide and black and gaping. I tried to back away, but my sledge trapped me on the breaking ice. I turned to my right, and then toward the ship, and in a moment, I was tangled in the traces. A whale's eye, like a yellow stone, peered up at me through the water. Then the head came crashing through the ice.

The floe tilted. I nearly lost my balance. I could look right into the whale's mouth, past its rows of teeth and down its wide, open throat. I could smell its breath, foul and fishy.

All around, the whales shoved their heads above the ice. They hovered there, looking at the dogs, at me, at Mr. Ponting, who was safe on thicker ice, kneeling down to catch his breath. I saw Mr. Meares leaping over the ice toward his dogs. The whale in front of me turned its eye slowly around and glared with a look that made my blood as cold as snow.

Then Mr. Keohane was there, his hand in my halter. "Come along, lad," he said, pulling gently. Even now his voice was soft and whispery. But it was tinged with fear.

The ice trembled. The whale sank below it, and the heads of all the others disappeared as well. I waited for a boom underneath me, for a loud crack and the split in the ice that would drop me into the sea, with Mr. Keohane clinging to my halter.

It never happened. The whales vanished, as if called away

by a voice I couldn't hear. The bits of ice slowly closed together, and the dogs curled up again, pressed against each other into one big ball of fur. Mr. Meares went away, and Mr. Keohane helped me toward the ship. And soon it was as though the killer whales had never come at all.

It is now January 12, 1911. Captain Scott records in his diary that the last load has been brought ashore from the Terra Nova. Only the meat remains, waiting for the men to finish chipping caves into the ice to be their storage rooms.

It's midsummer, and the sun never sets. Yesterday a blizzard blew up, and now the land is covered with white drifts. The temperature is falling to fifteen degrees.

Above the beach, on the flank of smoking Mount Erebus, the hut that will house the team through the winter is nearly finished. A stable, made of walls of straw bales, butts against one side. Now the ship's carpenter is building a darkroom in one corner for the photographer. He's putting in a desk for the captain, and a workstation for the meteorologists.

The hut is fifty feet long, divided not quite in the middle by a wall of crates. Scott, sticking to the navy tradition that he's known most of his life, is keeping the enlisted men separate from the officers.

He is cheerful and optimistic. He notes in his journal, "We are LANDED eight days after our arrival—a very good record."

❄ ❄ ❄

But Amundsen is catching up. The Norwegian is now working his way through the ice, and for him it goes quickly. Leads open ahead of the Fram, and the ship moves steadily forward. "A four days' pleasure trip," Amundsen calls it.

On January 11, as Scott sits out his first blizzard, Amundsen sights the Barrier from the deck of the Fram. He is closing in on the Bay of Whales, now just a hundred miles away.

But suddenly, things look grim for Amundsen. The bay is clogged with sea ice, and there is no chance of getting in. He scouts to the east, then returns in the morning. And as he watches, the ice floes in the bay begin to move. "One after another they came sailing out," he writes later. "The passage was soon free."

On January 14, he lands on the Barrier, on that enormous slab of floating ice, and begins to look for a place to build his hut. His 97 dogs have now become 116, and he brings them all ashore.

By his choice of a landing spot, Amundsen has leapfrogged ahead of Scott. He is sixty miles nearer to the Pole.

CHAPTER FOUR

THE very last thing to come off the ship was a small piano. I hauled it myself, in pieces, over the ice and up to the hut on its little hill twelve feet above the sea. I didn't know that.it was a piano until the men put it together and played a song. They seemed so happy then, everyone sunburned and smiling. That Captain Scott, he thought of everything.

There was a fire in the hut's stove, and smoke wafting from the roof. The sea sparkled with sunlight, dotted with floating castles of ice. It was a very beautiful place, everywhere white and snowy except for the strip of black sand along the shore. Mountains all around us, glaciers tumbling to the sea. And our stable! It might have come from a fairy tale: a stable built of straw.

I thought our work had ended for a while. But as soon as

we finished taking things *off* the ship, we started putting them *on* instead. Poor Weary Willy—who thought he'd earned a long rest—looked even more miserable than usual when he saw what we had to do. Over the ice we went again, but this time hauling rocks. It seemed stupid to fill a ship with rocks, but I imagined the men had a reason. They worked very hard to dig out the stones from the slopes above the beach, then ran them down icy chutes to the frozen sea, where they piled them on our sledges.

The motor sledges were put aboard next, then the dogs and all their gear. The pony sledges followed, and our harnesses and fodder. Mr. Meares went aboard, and Captain Scott as well. When the pony box was swung out from the deck, I thought all of us were moving on to somewhere else. But only Jehu and a pony named Chinaman were hoisted aboard. Then the box was stowed away again and the men gathered up the anchors and the mooring lines.

It made me sad to see that Jehu was leaving without me. I stood as close to the ship as I could get, and we whinnied sadly back and forth, not knowing if we'd ever see each other again. Then the killer whales came snorting along the edge of the ice, and Mr. Keohane led me away.

"Now, now, don't you worry, old friend," he said, petting my nose. "The ship is only going around the glacier. We're not being left behind."

No one had ever said anything nicer. I was his friend! After that, I couldn't think of him as a mister anymore. From then on, he was only Patrick.

❄ ❄ ❄

Just after Jehu left the winter station, so did I. But while he sailed on the ship, I went on foot. Along with six other ponies, with my friend Patrick at my side, I headed south.

A few miles ahead of us, a glacier stretched far out into the sea. It made such a dreadful wall of ice that no pony could ever cross it. So we went around its tip instead, out on the floating ice, while the ship sailed around to meet us.

We had no sledges. We just walked with our handlers, a line of ponies and men. As we started off, we passed the hut where Uncle Bill was standing. He was eager to come along, but he was tethered to a post and could only watch us pass with a sad, bewildered look. Then his handler—the lovely Birdie Bowers—came out from the hut to wave to us all. His enormous nose made a big shadow on the wall. "I'll be along in a moment," he shouted. "I've one more job to do."

Birdie Bowers always had "one more job to do." His job was looking after the supplies, and to me he was just like a raven, small and powerful, always thinking, and happiest when he had a collection of things around him.

We stayed as close to the shore as we could. The ice creaked and groaned, but we kept on going. I understood why our sledges had been taken on the ship. The ice was slowly breaking up, its little floes and islands drifting apart, sailing out to sea. In a way, we were racing the ice, trying to cross it before it vanished.

A layer of fresh snow hid holes big enough to swallow a pony, and the killer whales lurked along the edges. I was afraid every moment that one of them would come bursting up beside me, or that I would sink right through the ice.

Mr. Oates made us walk very slowly. "If a pony falls into one of these holes, I shall sit down and cry," he said.

A moment later, Guts shrieked. I turned my head and saw him on his stomach, as though his legs had been chopped away. His breath went out of him with a great *whoof!* as he landed. But already he was struggling to get up again, as the voices of the whales creaked in the ice. He paddled frantically in his little hole of slush and snow, but the more he moved, the more he sank. His whole back end disappeared into swirling water.

I heard the puff of a whale's breath. I saw the smoke it made, the little cloud on the sea, then the curve of its black fin sinking.

Guts flailed with his forelegs, driving himself deeper. In a moment, only his head and shoulders were left. The men were running to help him, crowding around, everyone trying to grab on to halter and tether or mane. But Guts was thrashing around so violently that no one could get close enough. Then someone found a rope and got a loop around his neck and forelegs. The sailors heaved together, dragging Guts from his hole. They pulled him out, wet and trembling, and gave him a bit of a rubdown before we headed off again.

We passed the tip of the glacier and saw the ship anchored a few miles ahead, near a cape of rock and snow. Smoke wafted from its funnel. As we made our way toward it, I heard someone coming behind us, a hurried thud of hooves and feet. It was Uncle Bill, half dragging poor Birdie Bowers. The man was wearing so many clothes that he looked as round as an egg. His face was fire-bright and slick with sweat. He'd put on his hat and his wind helmet, his parka, his sweaters, and three pairs of trousers, all to cross a bit of ice on a summer day. "It didn't feel fair to make the pony carry my clothes," he said. "So I wore my whole kit." That made everyone laugh. Uncle Bill was so big that he could have carried the whole man without slowing down at all.

Smoke thickened from the ship's funnel. I heard the sounds of motors and pulleys; I saw a group of men getting down to work. By the time we reached the ship, the motor sledges and the dogs had been unloaded. Captain Scott was helping Mr. Meares and the Russian harness their teams. Crates of supplies were swung down to the ice, but not Jehu. Not Chinaman.

From the ship came even more things than we'd unloaded at the wintering station. All our sledges and our gear, food and tents and oil—everything I could imagine came out of the ship and down to the ice. There was so much that we spent three days hauling it all to shore, and what a tremendous pile it made! The oats and fodder alone weighed more than fifteen thousand pounds.

When the ship was empty, it sailed off to the east to explore a new land, taking Jehu and Chinaman with it. Eight of us were left to tackle that pile of supplies. One load at a time, we hauled it around a ridge of ice, up a slope, up another, and on across the Barrier. The work was dreadfully difficult. We had only five miles to go to reach the Barrier, but getting there took forever. The snow was deep, the surface hard enough to hold a man or dog, but not a pony. I kept sinking to my knees or deeper, wading through snow with my sledge bogged behind me. Uncle Bill and Guts surged their way through it, but for me and the other smaller ponies, it was a trial. I floundered badly because I couldn't lift my legs clear of the snow. The more I fell behind, the harder I tried to catch up.

By the time we finished, I'd walked nearly a hundred miles, back and forth, with all my many trips.

❄   ❄   ❄

At the top of the first slope, on a bit of snow-covered ground, stood an old and lonely hut. It was smaller than the one we'd built at the winter station. It looked long abandoned and now was stuffed full of snow and ice because someone had left a window open. But there was still food on the table, and more on the shelves, and signs of men all around, as if they'd heard us coming and run away to hide. Patrick found a tin of gingerbread that was crisp and sweet. Captain Scott discovered dinner rolls that had been put down half finished, and still had teeth marks in them.

I could tell that Captain Scott had been there before, that he had lived in the hut for a while. But other people had come and gone since he'd left it, and he was angry at things they had done. It made him sad and silent as he stood in the doorway, as if he was looking at ghosts.

On the sheltered side of the hut were footprints in the snow, where the wind had not swept them away. I snuffled around, wondering if I might find forgotten biscuits, or apples frozen solid. Instead, I found the marks of pony hooves pressed deeply into old drifts.

That was a curious thing. Disturbing. I didn't like to think that other ponies had been to this frozen world and now had disappeared. I wished the men would tell me who had brought them, and what had happened in the end. But no one did.

❄   ❄   ❄

It was late when we left the lonely hut with our first loads, heading south again. We struggled up to the Barrier, that huge, vast plain of snow and ice. It stretched farther than I could see, and its barren whiteness scared me. I kept looking sideways at the mountains on my right, glad they were nearby but afraid they would soon fade away. The men marked our path by building cairns of snow.

We traveled just half a mile more until Captain Scott blew on a whistle, and the man in the lead swung to the side with his pony. The rest of us followed, all turning out to the left, till we stood in a line sideways to our trail. As men set up their tents, our handlers stretched a picket line between two sledges and tied us to it with our tethers. They gave us food and blankets before they went away to their meals.

This was our first camp on the Barrier, and what a very cold place it was. I stood with my tail to the wind, watching Patrick's tent. I never took my eyes away from it until he emerged in the morning.

The second day was worse. We went back with our empty sledges and brought more supplies up onto the Barrier. It was fine until we pushed past our old camp. Then we came into a big patch of soft snow, and I sank right into it. For half a mile, all of us floundered along. But I had the worst time of it, and the other ponies passed me. When the snow grew solid again, I tried too hard to catch up. I tripped and sprained an ankle.

It was sudden. A jolt of pain burned through my leg and I fell forward onto my chest. Patrick, beside me, looked startled. "James, what's wrong?" he said.

I didn't want him to see that I was hurt. An injured pony was a dead pony; I had seen it a hundred times. So I clambered up and stood wobbling for a moment, trying not to cry out as I waited for the pain to go away. I ate some snow, though it chilled me right through. Then I pulled at the traces and tugged the sledge forward, hoping no one would notice my lameness.

But Patrick looked at me strangely. "You're limping," he said.

I tried to keep going, but he wouldn't let me. He held my halter and called out loudly, "Captain Oates!"

His voice drifted away across the Barrier, soaked up by the snow and the sky. He shouted again, "Sir, my pony can't walk!"

Far ahead, leading Punch, Mr. Oates stopped and looked back. Patrick waved to him with wide sweeps of his arm.

As much as I wanted to go on, it was a relief to stop walking. Big Uncle Bill was nearly a quarter of a mile ahead by then. He turned his head to see me. So did Weary Willy— much closer. So did Blucher and Guts and Blossom. But they all kept hauling through the snow. I didn't expect them to stop, because there was nothing they could do. We had known all of our lives—or all the years we'd spent with men—what it meant to go lame.

I stared at Mr. Oates as he came trudging toward me. He

didn't have a gun in his hand—not yet—but he didn't look at me or at anyone else. Patrick rubbed my cheek with his bare knuckles. "It will be all right, James Pigg," he said.

I knew he was trying to be kind. I pressed against him, and he pressed back.

I was sad. I didn't want to be shot there in the sunshine, in that soft white snow. But I didn't blame the men for what they had to do. This wasn't their fault; it was mine. I felt sorry for Mr. Oates, and especially for Captain Scott because I'd let him down so badly. I wondered what he'd say when he heard the gunshot. I could almost hear his voice. *"Poor James Pigg. He was a good lad."*

Patrick kept petting me. Mr. Oates joined us, puffing his breaths in the cold. He pulled his gloves away with his teeth, squatted beside me, and lifted my sore foot.

"I think he twisted something," said Patrick. "But he'll be all right, won't he, sir? A bit of a rest will sort him out?"

Mr. Oates kept pressing and poking at my tendons. "I doubt that very much," he said.

"But he's barely begun," said Patrick with a small laugh. "He *has* to be all right."

Mr. Oates stood up. He squinted at the sun, at the lonely Barrier stretching south. When he reached into his jacket, I closed my eyes so that I wouldn't have to see the gun.

It was a hard thing to stand there and wait for the end. I heard the ponies struggling ahead, the dogs barking in the distance. Then I smelled tobacco and dared to take a look. And there was Mr. Oates with his pipe in his hand—not a gun. He lit it slowly, with nearly as much smoke as a steam engine, staring at me all that time.

"We could lighten his load, I suppose," he said. "Give him a rest tomorrow. Maybe that will help."

Patrick looked delighted. So was I, of course, but he didn't really know that. He freed me from the traces and we walked very slowly together. He kept his hand firmly in my halter. "Come on, lad," he said. "You'll be getting to the Pole."

To the Pole! I didn't really understand exactly. I pictured an actual pole somewhere very far away, a bit of wood standing lonely on the ice. I had no idea just then how far there was to go, or what troubles lay ahead. It wouldn't have mattered anyway. I wanted to stay with Patrick, and now that I had his promise to take me to the Pole, I had no fear of being left behind.

I limped along beside him.

The men were cheerful, excited to be at the beginning of a big journey. They chattered all the time and laughed a lot as we plodded on. They pointed out every little thing, making sure every man shared each excitement. Someone spotted two strange mounds in the snow, and didn't they wonder about that! They peered at them through telescopes, muttering away in their groups like the penguins on the ice. Then Captain Scott went over to have a look.

We saw him bend down and brush the snow with his mittens. Then he pulled up scraps of old cloth, and wooden sticks, and something that sparkled in the sun.

"Good Lord, they're tents!" said Birdie Bowers.

He was right. Out there on the Barrier, buried and forgotten, a pair of tents stood flapping in the wind where men had stopped and ate and slept.

The sparkling thing was a stove. Captain Scott got it going, and he cooked a meal from the things in the tent: cocoa and Bovril, sheeps' tongue, cheese and biscuits. I was offered one of the biscuits by Patrick. It disappointed him badly when I wouldn't take it, but I didn't feel like eating. The wind blew gritty snow across the Barrier, and the men sat with their backs to the blow, eating food that I thought belonged to ghosts.

We pushed on a little farther, then stopped to make camp. Patrick offered me a biscuit again, and this time I took it. He smiled as I ate. At the other end of the picket line, Birdie Bowers was feeding biscuits to Uncle Bill, because he was worried about *him* as well. "He's having trouble with his forefeet," said Birdie. Even the biggest pony was struggling, so I didn't feel so bad.

Mr. Oates made me rest the next day while the other ponies brought up more supplies. It was awful to be left behind and see them trek off through the snow. But my leg was very sore, and in truth I was glad for the rest. In my old home in the forest, I would have been kept at work until I finally fell in my tracks. That would have been hard to bear, but all I'd expect. I had believed it was the way to the ponies' place, that I could never get there by shirking.

Hours and hours went by before I heard the ponies coming back, their sledges rasping in the snow, their breaths hot and panting. I felt lonely then, afraid they'd be angry because I hadn't done my share. But Blossom came and nibbled at me, picking away my lice, and I knew that no one minded that I had stayed behind.

In the morning it was Sunday, and Captain Scott held a service on the Barrier, with all the men standing silently as he read from a small black book. The wind whooshed across the ice, and snow flurried around their feet, but they didn't move until Captain Scott had finished and they had sung a solemn song.

Mr. Oates handed out bandages to the pony handlers. He showed them how to wrap our legs like soldiers'—round and round—so the snow crust wouldn't chafe our skin every time we stepped through it. Uncle Bill didn't understand, and right away he ate one of his bandages. I thought mine would be a big help, but for days I did very little work as we moved the supplies forward again, to a place about two miles from the sea.

Two men were sent back with injuries, and Captain Scott took Nobby for himself. We moved along in stages, back and forth across the Barrier, every journey a struggle. There was ice as hard as rock, then snow as soft as pudding, and we wallowed in drifts up to our bellies. We had to leap at the traces then and jerk the sledges forward. Our legs ached; our shoulders ached. We sweated as we moved along, and shivered when we stopped, with our sweat freezing into skins of ice.

My eyes stung from the light on the snow. When the sky was clear and the surface glared, I had to squint as hard as I could. But cloudy days were even worse. The white of the sky and the white of the snow were the same, and it was hard to place my hooves on ground that had no shadows. There were times I could hardly see anything, but still I soldiered on.

I wasn't happy that my sledge was the lightest of all. It was hard to think that I wasn't doing my share, and I wished that

Jehu and Chinaman were with me, so that I wouldn't be the weakest of all.

When Captain Scott blew his whistle that afternoon and called an end to the march, I had never been more tired. I gobbled down the biscuits that Patrick fed me. The dogs got into a big, happy fight with each other, but the ponies just stood and panted clouds of breath.

Captain Scott went ahead on his skis to see if the way ahead was any better. But he came back very disappointed. "It looks grim," he told Mr. Oates, who was looking rather gloomy. "What do you think?"

"It's too much for the ponies," said Mr. Oates. "They won't last long like this."

"Let's give the snowshoes a go," said the captain.

Mr. Oates let out his breath. "They're a wasted effort, those wretched things."

"Nonetheless, I should like to try," said Captain Scott, and he sent Birdie Bowers to fetch them.

Birdie could normally put his fingers on anything in a moment, but not this time. After a lot of rummaging around, he produced just one set of snowshoes. They were the strangest things I'd ever seen: hoops of wire and bamboo that looked like squashed umbrellas. I was sure Mr. Oates was right and that I would tangle my feet together as soon as I wore them. So I was happy when the men chose Weary Willy to try them out.

That sad old pony looked pretty sorry for himself as the men strapped on the shoes. It was a young man who led him off, a Norwegian named Gran who'd been brought along to teach the others how to ski.

Weary Willy moved pretty slowly at first, looking down at his feet with such a woeful expression that Cherry fell laughing into a snowbank. But Weary got the hang of it quickly, and soon went strolling across drifts that had swallowed him before. It was magic, I thought. The snowshoes had a power that could hold up a pony. I wondered if Weary Willy could walk on clouds if he wore those shoes, or climb the back of a rainbow.

Captain Scott was very pleased. "Now we can double our distance," he said happily. "Break out the rest of them, Birdie."

But there *were* no more, and that crushed him. Poor Birdie Bowers, who might have counted every grain of rice, was beside himself trying to understand how snowshoes had been left behind.

"Well, never mind," said Captain Scott. He sent two men on a dogsled all the way back to Cape Evans, to the winter station where we'd first come ashore. He told them to hurry, because the ice was already breaking up.

They went racing away in a mad barking of dogs, the little sledge tipping over the drifts. They disappeared behind a wave of snow, then rose to the top of the next one, the dogs dashing along in their double line. On the white ground, with the clouds behind them, it seemed as though they were flying.

We were more than twenty miles from the winter station. The dog drivers were gone until noon the next day, when they arrived in the usual clamor of shouts and barks. It always startled me to hear the Russian words from the drivers. The sound carried me back with a flash of fear to my days in the forest with men who broke bottles on my bones.

Captain Scott and the others hurried out to meet the drivers, but the sledge was empty. The sea ice had broken up so much that the men had never reached the winter station.

For Captain Scott, it was a hard blow—"a bitter pill," he'd say. I saw him stare out across the Barrier, at the hundreds of miles we had to go, and he seemed a little bit beaten. He went into his tent and wrote in his journal, and we didn't move on that day at all.

The temperature fell in the night—or what *passed* as the night. The sun swooped very low but never disappeared, and when our shadows were their longest, the melted snow froze up again.

In the morning, we started out ahead of the dogs. They were faster, but they liked to have a trail to follow, so Captain Scott held them back to give us a head start.

When Patrick harnessed me to my sledge in the morning, my leg still hurt. I worried about falling through the drifts again. So I watched Weary Willy go ahead on the snowshoes. He did even better than he had before. Why, he went at a trot, and that was a rare thing for Weary. Then Uncle Bill went behind him—and with his first step on the snow, he broke through the crust. But he was the heaviest pony, and the rest of us managed all right. The frozen snow was so hard that Weary didn't need the shoes, and someone took them off.

Poor Uncle Bill didn't like to follow; he wanted to be in front of everyone, where a leader belonged. So he tried to hurry, and that made him sink deeper. And the more he sank, the more he hurried. An hour later, he was drenched with sweat, as sleek and shiny as a seal. We all passed him. Even I went past him, though I didn't want to. It was hard to go ahead of the leader.

We went five miles in not much more than an hour. Then the sun was high again, and the snow began to thaw, and we started falling through the crust again. So Captain Scott blew his whistle, and we wheeled off to the left like soldiers.

We were all tied along the picket line—our harnesses off, our blankets on—before Uncle Bill came staggering into the camp. He smashed through the snow, his magnificent mane all matted with sweat.

Captain Scott watched him panting. "We should have put the shoes on that one, Birdie," he said.

Mr. Bowers nodded.

"Well, tomorrow."

"I'm afraid not," said Mr. Bowers. "Don't you know? The shoes were left behind."

"What?" The captain was frowning. "Who decided that?"

Birdie shrugged. He looked uncomfortable, as though he knew who had done it but didn't want to say. Then Captain Scott looked around, and I was glad that Mr. Oates didn't see the icy look that was aimed toward him. It would certainly have hurt his feelings, because Mr. Oates meant nothing but the best for the ponies. If he left the shoes behind—and I wasn't sure he did—it was only because he felt they would bring more grief than help.

Captain Scott sent Gran skiing back to get them. Then he gathered all the men, including Mr. Oates, and gave a little talk. "A change of plans," he told them. There would be no more shuffling back and forth. Instead, he would load our sledges heavily and lead us steadily south for two weeks. We would build small caches along the way and plant one enormous depot at 80 degrees south latitude. That was more than two hundred miles away, and we had to get there and back before the southern summer ended. In springtime, when we all set out in a dash toward the Pole, the food we had cached along the route would feed ponies and dogs.

When everyone agreed to that, the captain had one more suggestion. "This snow is too soft for the ponies," he said. "I suggest we travel at night, when the surface is hardest."

There was no argument. Mr. Oates, always thinking of his animals, said it was a splendid idea. The ponies could rest in the warmest part of the day instead of coming off the march all lathered with sweat, to spend the night shivering.

"Then it's settled. We'll start tonight," said Captain Scott.

The men pitched their tents and disappeared inside to eat and rest. I sometimes thought that men were like beavers: They liked to stay inside a little house, and when they came out, they went straight to work, always very busy. I had seldom seen a man or a beaver doing absolutely nothing.

We marched for three hours that night, ate dinner, and marched for two more. We covered ten miles before the snow softened and Uncle Bill suddenly fell through.

The ponies close behind him blundered into the hole he

made, and there was soon a big pileup of ponies and sledges, such a tangle that the animals had to be unharnessed. Patrick led me far to the right, where the snow was still hard, so I pulled my sledge right to the camp, proud that I could do my share.

As we turned off the trail, Patrick smiled. "Why, James Pigg," he said. "You're not limping, you see."

I actually looked down at my legs, watching my front hooves swing forward. The bad one didn't even hurt anymore.

"Good lad!" cried Patrick, with a friendly thump on my shoulder. We walked in together, side by side, and Captain Scott grinned when he saw that I was better.

I wouldn't have minded going back to help with the sledges. But it was Uncle Bill they chose for that. They put the shoes on him, and he trekked back and forth, doing the work for all the others. He thought he was being punished, but it only made sense for the strongest pony to wear the shoes.

He was bringing in the last sledge when the dog teams arrived. They swept into the camp, over a rise and past the place where the ponies had floundered. They came barking louder than usual, a sign that they were tired and hungry.

Captain Scott walked over to meet Mr. Meares, who was driving the first team, riding—like a Russian—on his sledge. The dogs were thin as rakes, hungry and mean. They looked dangerous to me, but Captain Scott didn't notice. He kept walking. The dogs snarled at him, and suddenly the dog Osman swept around and grabbed the captain by his ankle.

It was an awful moment. The dog thrashed its head. Captain Scott fell to the snow. He tried to crawl away but couldn't. He tried to kick the dog, but it held on, growling like mad. The other dogs were closing in on him now, their teeth gleaming in hungry grins, the hair standing like spikes on their backs.

A dog was heartless. To a dog, a man was no different than a biscuit, something to be gobbled down if there was even half a chance of doing it. The team was a pack, and it moved against Captain Scott, every dog intent on tearing off his own little bit of the meal.

Mr. Meares leapt from his sledge. He struck at the dogs with his driving stick, trying to chase them off. It seemed at first they wouldn't go. They turned on him as well with the same growls and snarls, their faces twisted into looks of evil.

But Mr. Meares wasn't scared. He waded right in among them, swinging his stick, kicking out with his feet. There was never a greater coward than a dog, and soon the growls turned to yelps and whines, and the beasts sulked away with their tails bent down.

Mr. Meares saved his last blows for the dog Osman. I thought he might beat the thing to death—and I wouldn't have minded—but Captain Scott shouted at him to stop.

I could hardly believe it. There was the captain sprawled on the snow with his boot nearly torn away, crying out to save the dog that had nearly killed him. "It's instinct," he said. "You can't break them of instinct."

That was the way of Captain Scott. If the dogs had ripped him to shreds, if they'd torn off his legs and his hands and his arms, and if the only thing left was his head, he might still have spoken up and said, "They're just hungry." He thought he understood the thinking of dogs, believing their lives were ruled by fear and food and nothing else. He didn't trust them, and he didn't like them very much. But he was still as kindly to a dog as he was to a pony.

※　※　※

I lost track of the miles we traveled, of the times we camped, of the cairns that were built by the men to mark our path. My eyes got so sore and dim that they couldn't make sense of things sometimes. The whole Barrier seemed to slope uphill, while enormous ridges rose in our path, only to shrink into tiny waves as we reached them. The snow enjoyed playing little tricks.

For most of a week, we marched to the southeast, with the smoking mountain falling away behind us. Then we came to a place that Captain Scott named Corner Camp. To me it looked just like all the other places where we'd stopped to pitch the tents. But Captain Scott said it marked our turning point. He held out his arm and pointed to the Pole, still hundreds of miles in the distance. From then on, we would head straight for the south, he said.

At Corner Camp we buried bales of fodder and many pounds of supplies. Then a blizzard came howling down from the mountains, and for three days it kept blowing. The wind was so full of snow that I could barely see Blucher beside me, and nothing at all beyond him. Like tiny pebbles flung against us, the snow pelted my ears and eyes and nose. It tore at the tents with a fluttering boom of canvas.

I was very cold. My hair still thought it was summer and had never grown its winter thickness. The blanket helped, but snow was driven underneath it, piling up against my skin. My ears were sore and prickly, and I was afraid that my tail would be torn away.

I didn't sleep for more than a moment at a time, and I envied the dogs for their little nests below the snow. They dug themselves in at the start of the blizzard and didn't come out until it was over.

If not for Mr. Oates, I might have given up. He came often to see us, groping from the blizzard like a blind man. Sometimes Cherry came with him, and sometimes Patrick. Though they walked only a few yards from the tents, they arrived white from head to toe. With helmets on their heads, and mittens on their hands, only tiny bits of their faces could be seen. They brought oil cakes and biscuits, but I was too cold to be hungry.

When the blizzard finally ended, we got on our way again. The men took down their tents and dug out the sledges. The dogs heard the sounds and *exploded* from the snow, bursting from their little burrows.

Soon the sun was shining. The Barrier glittered in all directions as the men took down the picket line. They peeled away our blankets, tied the snowshoes onto Uncle Bill's broad hooves, and walked us into our harnesses.

Then Captain Scott looked around. Satisfied, he nodded. "All right, Bowers," he shouted. "Go ahead."

The little man turned the big pony south onto the trail. Uncle Bill stepped out happily, steady on his snowshoes. One by one we followed in his trail, leaving the dogs and their drivers behind. At the back of the line, Captain Scott walked with old Nobby.

It was good to be moving. But the blizzard had turned

the Barrier to mush, and I struggled again through the drifts. We all looked slumped and slow and tired, beaten by the storm. I could see Blossom's ribs bending as he breathed. But Captain Scott said things would improve, and they did. The snow grew firm as we went along, and for three days we pushed to the south.

Far to the right were the mountains, but I hardly ever saw them. They liked to hide in the glare of the sun, or in the whirls of snow, or in the mist and fog. So I saw mostly whiteness, no matter what the weather.

It was hard going. A never-ending wind blew in our faces. It snatched up the snow from the Barrier and swept it along in a stinging cloud. I longed for the sheltering trees of the forest, for bushes or valleys, for anything that would block that wind.

I started falling behind. Patrick never made me hurry, but when I heard Blucher behind me, wheezing along in my trail, I had to move faster to keep ahead of him.

Blucher was in a bad way. His load of fodder and biscuits was lightened to four hundred pounds, then halved to just two hundred. But even that was almost too much for him, and on the third day after the blizzard, his handler—a kindly sailor named Mr. Forde—let him walk the last few yards to the camp as he hauled the sledge himself.

When Captain Scott blew his whistle to end the march, I staggered from the trail. I knew the routine so well, I hardly noticed. The men tied the same picket line to the same two sledges, and tethered us along it in the same order. Other men were setting up the tents, exactly as I'd seen them do it again and again. On went our blankets, out came our food, just as I knew would happen.

Then everything changed.

Instead of heading for his tent, Captain Scott started digging in the snow. I watched him as I chewed an oatcake, trying to puzzle out what he was doing. I wondered if there was grass below the snow, the tart and frozen stems that I had loved to browse in the forest. I moved closer, to the end of my tether.

But the only thing Captain Scott dug from the snow was a block of snow. He set it down on the surface and dug up another.

All the ponies were watching him. The men all watched as well. They were cold and tired and hungry, eager to get into their tents and cook their dinners. But they stayed to watch.

Captain Scott went quietly on with his work. He arranged the blocks to build a little wall in front of Nobby, to shield his pony from the wind.

It was the nicest thing I had ever seen a man do for an animal. He went to a lot of trouble to see that Nobby was comfortable before he found comfort himself. And from then on, every man did the same thing. At the end of every march, Patrick built a wall for me, Mr. Oates for Punch, that lovely Birdie for Uncle Bill. They built half the wall as soon we stopped, and the rest when they finished their dinners.

It was wonderful. I loved to stand behind my wall and watch the wind whip whirls of snow from the top of it. At last I could sleep.

But some of the ponies were angry at the men for bringing them out on the Barrier. Guts, especially, liked to kick down his wall just so poor Cherry would have to come out and build it again. He did everything he could to make sure the men suffered too.

＊　＊　＊

South we went. South again, every day a little worse. Our sledges grew a tiny bit lighter every time we ate, for it meant that much less to carry. But I was sure that mine was growing heavier! Soft snow on the Barrier made the work harder for everybody.

Blucher and Blossom looked half dead as they struggled along with their sledges. Their noses nearly touched the snow, and their hooves never lifted free of it. They dragged long furrows from one footstep to another.

Now it was Weary Willy who lagged behind, way at the back of the line. He wasn't tired as much as lazy, and just went as slowly as he could until he heard the shrill of Captain Scott's whistle. And didn't he move himself then! He went along at a trot almost, his mane shaking, his harness buckles jingling.

His trick nearly did him in one day as a keen wind tore across the Barrier.

We were moving very slowly into whirls of blowing snow; our line stretched out for more than half a mile. I couldn't see Uncle Bill; he was too far ahead. Only Weary Willy was behind me. I could just see him, dim and gray, if I turned my head far enough.

Captain Scott blew his whistle early. The sound was muffled by the snow, so faint that I doubted if Weary Willy could hear it. I imagined him dragging his hooves, lagging farther behind every minute, not knowing he could hurry now and get his food and shelter.

At nearly the same moment, I heard the dogs. Every day, it gave me a fright as they came up along our trail, as though all day they'd been chasing us. Today their foolish yipping and yapping came more faintly than the whistle, the sound pushed away by the wind. Patrick didn't hear anything. It was no wonder, his head covered by his helmet and his helmet by his hat. He didn't look up at the whistle, or back at the dogs, but kept going at the same steady pace as if we had hours more to travel.

The dogs drew closer, their sound more frantic. They used the wild bark that told they were hungry.

I looked back at Weary. He was like a shadow on the snow as he plowed his way through a drift. I saw the dog Rabchick appear from the blizzard, bounding along at the head of his team. He was a wild sort of dog, that Rabchick; if his parents were not wolves, his grandparents were. The second and third dogs appeared behind him, then the third and the fourth, and they swung out in a line to pass the pony. I saw the sledge appear, and young Gran racing along with it.

Then Weary Willy stumbled in the drift, his back end collapsing. And quick as a wink, the dog Rabchick suddenly turned and went straight at him.

Patrick was tugging on my halter, trying to make me face forward. But he stopped when he heard the new sound of the dogs, the savage snarls and growls.

The snow thickened with a gust of wind. We saw only the shapes of the dogs and the man and the pony. In a pack, the dogs were attacking. Weary Willy struggled up and kicked with his hind legs as he bit with his teeth. He plucked a dog right from the snow and thrashed it around in the air. He hurled it down and snatched up another, whirling again as the dogs leapt for his withers.

Then Gran was there, wading into the fray, striking out with his ski pole. Mr. Meares appeared beside him with his dog stick, but the dogs kept attacking old Weary Willy. The pony was tangled now in his harness. He couldn't run away, and he couldn't turn anymore to face the dogs.

They went for his blind spots, for the backs of his legs. He kicked like a maniac; he snorted and screamed. Gran broke his ski pole on the back of a dog. Mr. Meares broke his stick on another. Both kept thrashing away with the shattered handles, until I thought the dogs would turn on *them*. One dog yelped, and then another, and that was enough for the rest. They gave up the fight and rolled onto their backs or slinked away. They whined the most pitiful whines I'd ever heard, as though they felt the world was terribly cruel.

I hoped the men would kill them. But they didn't. Captain Scott was just as pleased to see that no dog was injured as he was to see that Weary Willy wasn't eaten. The pony had nothing worse than a bit of scraped-away hair. But he'd put up a great fight, and the men rewarded him by harnessing themselves to his sledge and dragging it into the camp.

Captain Scott was one of those men, and he was furious to find how heavy that sledge really was. Weary Willy had been dragging more weight than any other pony. It was no wonder, I thought, that he'd become a little stubborn.

That night, in the long sun, Weary Willy was fed hot mash. He got a wall that was higher than usual, and extra sacking on top of his blankets. I shivered beside him as the temperature fell far below zero, and I wondered if he wasn't trying for sympathy by looking so pathetic.

❄   ❄   ❄

Ninety miles from where we'd started, the men had a meeting in one of the tents. I could see their shapes on the canvas as they sat around the cooking stove. It looked warm in there—a little room full of warmth on the endless snow of the Barrier. The stove hissed as it burned. Someone put a kettle on top, the shadow of his arm stretching out.

It was Captain Scott. I heard his voice. "The ponies are a disappointment," he said.

At the edge of the group, Mr. Oates leaned back until he rested his shoulders on the canvas. I could tell his shape right through the cloth. He answered quite loudly: "You expect too much of them."

Behind me on the picket line, Blucher was pawing at the snow. He looked thin and hungry, and I imagined that he was searching for grass where he couldn't possibly find any.

"I still want to get them to eighty degrees," said Captain Scott. The shadow of his hand turned the shadow of his kettle. "If we don't leave our depot at eighty degrees, we won't have a chance in the spring."

"Oh, you'll get them there," said Mr. Oates, with a cheery laugh. "Or most of them, at any rate. But I'll tell you this: You won't get them back."

The stove kept hissing away. Little whirls of steam shadowed on the side of the tent.

"There's three that might drop dead tomorrow," said Mr. Oates. "They're on their last legs. They're done in."

I looked again at Blucher. He was still muzzling through the snow, and I was happy he wasn't listening to the men or he didn't understand the words. He was surely one of the three who wouldn't last, and I thought Blossom was another. But I wasn't sure about the third.

Birdie Bowers looked at Captain Scott. I could tell it was him by the long shadow of his nose. "Why not send them back now?" he said. "They've done a sterling job, haven't they? Let them live to fight another day."

That was all I heard. Patrick came out from the other tent and began to feed me biscuits. Weary Willy put on such a show of sadness that he got one as well.

In the morning, I was surprised to see what happened.

Nearly a hundred miles from his hut, at 79 degrees south latitude, Captain Scott sends the weakest ponies back to the stable. He buries their load of fodder, names the place Bluff Depot, and keeps heading south with his five other ponies. He plans to reach 80 degrees and plant his final cache, a ton of supplies. Every pound of supplies that he carries now—every mile he takes it—means less work in the spring, a quicker dash to the Pole.

His dogs are thin, underfed on their diet of biscuits. He notes that Meares will have to give up his habit of riding on the sledge if he wants the dogs to last. "Meares, I think, rather imagined himself racing to the Pole and back on a dog sledge," he writes in his journal. "This journey has opened his eyes a good deal."

The ponies are worse. Cold weather is hard on the animals, and the temperature falls to twenty below out on the Barrier. To spare the animals, Scott stops early. He plants his last depot at 79 degrees, 28½ minutes south, about twenty miles short of his goal. He marks the spot well, with a cairn six feet high, a flag on a bamboo pole, and a pile of biscuit tins to reflect the sun. He stands the empty sledges up on end, then turns north for the trek home.

It's February 16, 1911.

❄   ❄   ❄

As Scott marches south, his Terra Nova sails along to the east. She's heading for the farthest edge of the Barrier, to an explored part of the continent. She carries four men and two ponies—Jehu and Chinaman—meaning to leave them in the strange land and collect them again the next summer.

But as the ship crosses the Bay of Whales, the men see a strange sight. The spars of a ship reach up above the edge of the Barrier, stark black lines of masts and yards against the glare of the sky.

They know right away it's the Fram. There's no other ship it can be.

Aboard the Fram, a watchman is drinking coffee. He hears a rattle of chain and comes up on deck at midnight to see the Terra Nova anchored off the stern. He rubs his eyes; he pinches himself, because he can hardly believe he's awake.

Amundsen visits the Terra Nova, then the Englishmen dine on the Fram. But the visits are short. Everyone seems in a hurry.

The Terra Nova changes plans and returns straight away to Evans. She brings the news that Amundsen is less than six hundred miles away, working his dogs on the ice.

She unloads the two ponies, who have no choice but to swim ashore, towed along by a whaleboat. Chinaman manages well, but Jehu can't move his legs and has to be hauled through a mile of icy water. On shore, each pony gets half a bottle of brandy poured down his throat, and Chinaman staggers around for a while, comically drunk. But the swim nearly kills little Jehu, and he's never the same after that.

❋   ❋   ❋

Amundsen is also laying depots on the Barrier. He has taken just three men, three sledges, and eighteen dogs. Each sledge carries 550 pounds, but most of that weight—350 pounds per sledge—is dog food.

A man goes ahead on skis, "to show the direction and encourage the dogs," he says. The sledges follow in a line. The lead driver has the compass, and he calls directions to the forerunner: "A little to the right, a little to the left." Each is annoyed by the other.

The forerunner has the hardest job. "It is no easy matter to go straight on a surface without landmarks," says Amundsen. "Imagine an immense plain that you have to cross in thick fog; it is dead calm, and the snow lies evenly, without drifts. What would you do? An Eskimo can manage it, but none of us."

Amundsen drives the last sledge, watching for things that fall from the others. They travel through a haze that hides the horizon. There are no shadows; the forerunner can't see the rises and hollows in the snow until he stumbles over them. But they make seventeen miles a day, then twenty-eight on day three. They reach 80 degrees south on Valentine's Day, and Amundsen places his depot there. He builds a cairn twelve feet high.

They mark their route with black flags. When the flags run out, they use dried fish instead, dangled from bamboo poles. Every half a kilometer—measured by the sledge meter—a man calls out the distance, and Amundsen drives another fish into the snow as they dash along. With their sledges emptied, they're flying over the Barrier: forty-three miles the first day, sixty-two the next, to reach their base in just two days.

It's autumn now in the south, with winter coming quickly. But Amundsen makes two more trips across the Barrier, laying depots as far to the south as 82 degrees of latitude.

He settles down for the winter with a huge lead over Scott. But he's worried that he might be beaten already. He knows the Englishmen have brought motor sledges, and he imagines the machines rattling on and on across the Barrier.

CHAPTER FIVE

I spent the night wondering about the third pony. I didn't sleep for all my thinking.

Blossom and Blucher were certainly crocks. They barely ate, and shivered all the time, and went everywhere at a plodding walk as slow as funeral horses. I was pleased they were turning back. But who would go with them? I had no idea. Was it Weary Willy? Was it Nobby?

In the end, I couldn't have been more surprised.

It was me.

I knew it as soon as Patrick came out of his tent. He was more quiet than usual, not joking with the others. He came and fed me a biscuit, as he always did. But as he brushed the snow from my blanket and mane, I could feel the sadness inside him. I heard him sigh as he looked to the north. I knew he was turning back, though he'd rather go on.

Right after breakfast, the men took the supplies from my sledge, from Blossom's and Blucher's, and buried it all in the snow. Captain Scott named the place Bluff Depot because there was a big bluff of mountains fifty miles to the east, though mostly it was hidden. They built a cairn to mark the place.

Then Patrick took off my blanket. "Come on, lad," he said. The sun had burned his face, except for two white circles around his eyes where his snow goggles usually rested. "Let's get you home now. Next year, it's the Pole."

So off I went with Blucher and Blossom, down our tracks toward the sea.

It was embarrassing to be sent back with the old wheezers. I couldn't believe that I was a wheezer too, a crock, not wanted on the depot journey. I reminded myself: "My name is James Pigg; I'm a good lad."

At least I led the way. That was something that made me feel a bit better. We had one sledge, and I did the pulling. It was almost empty, easy to haul with the wind behind me. Many times, I had to stop to let the others catch up.

Blucher was behind me. His handler, the kindly Mr. Forde, seemed to be holding him up as they walked along together, each leaning on the other. Both had their heads down, their feet dragging. At the back was Blossom, not much better, led by Mr. Teddy. I felt sad to see those ponies struggling on. I remembered them rolling on the ice on the day we'd come ashore. In the sunshine and the cold, they had frolicked like colts. And now—not quite a month later—they could hardly walk. They couldn't even lift their heads. The only thing they ever saw was the snow right in front of them.

I was reminded again and again of the old mare lagging at the back of the herd when I was young. I saw it in the way Blucher breathed, in the way Blossom's ears sagged like ferns in the fall. I wondered if they would take themselves off alone if they had the chance, the way the mare had done, to die on the lonely Barrier. I couldn't imagine doing it myself. How brave and desperate would a creature have to be for that?

I felt tired too, of course. Deep inside, I was still so chilled by the blizzards that I thought my middle might never warm up. There was a little part of me—maybe in my heart—that was happy because I was heading for the stable.

The men seldom spoke. It was Mr. Teddy who set the pace because he was an officer, the second in command of the whole expedition. His real name was Teddy Evans, and he had the same last name as the big sailor Taff Evans, and that was very confusing. So I thought of him as Mr. Teddy instead.

It was funny that all three of our handlers were sailors. Now they walked on frozen water that floated on the sea, and that seemed a strange thing. I saw Mr. Teddy pop a little piece of biscuit into Blossom's mouth, and I wondered what it was about sailors that made them so kind to animals.

The sky was full of churning clouds when we set off. But soon a blizzard whirled up from behind us, turning everything to frozen white.

The cold and the misery were too much for little Blucher. His legs wobbled, and down he went in a heap. Mr. Forde knelt beside him in the snow. "Come on, Blucher," he said. "Please. Come on." He pushed and pulled and got the pony up again, and for a moment, it seemed that Blucher might re-cover. He walked on a few yards with Mr. Forde holding his halter, telling him, "There you go. That's good." But again he toppled over, and now it took all three of the men to get him on his feet.

We stopped there. We went no farther. The men built a wall, and in its shelter they kept rubbing Blucher's legs. They tried to feed him, to walk him back and forth. Their faces froze in the wind, but they kept at it. They did everything they could possibly do, yet they couldn't save Blucher. The pony collapsed into a small and quivering heap.

"He's done," said Mr. Teddy. "I'm sorry, Forde, but the most kindly thing is to help him on his way."

Mr. Forde nodded. He was crying, his tears freezing on his cheeks in jagged, windblown lines. He took out his sailor's knife, shook off his mitts, and opened it. Blucher was on his side, his chest heaving.

"I'll do it," said Patrick, holding out his hand for the knife.

But Mr. Forde wouldn't let him. "No, no, he's *my* pony," he said. "I've looked after him this long; I'll look after him now."

It was over in a moment, as the blizzard swept across the Barrier with a melancholy moan. Poor Blucher was so old, so small and sick, that there was almost no blood to come out of him. Mr. Forde held the pony's head, the two of them stretched out on the snow, and I felt such a terrible sadness in the air that I thought it would hang over this place forever.

The blizzard seemed longer and colder than the one be-fore. It buried the sledge and it buried the tent, and it buried little Blucher, bit by bit, until only his silver mane fluttered above the Barrier. Then that was buried too, and there was only the snow where he lay.

Behind the pony wall, Blossom and I huddled close together. Under two blankets, he was shaking like a mouse, swaying his head from side to side. I pressed against him as hard as I could, trying to make him warmer.

When the sky finally cleared, the men buried Blucher. The wind was still keen and cold, whipping up funnels of snow. In their heavy, furry clothes, the men built a little cairn to mark the grave. They stuck a flagstaff into the snow, and we went along to the north.

❄   ❄   ❄

The wind seemed colder now. Blowing snow whirled through the air all around us. It was Blossom who lagged behind, Blossom who slowed us down. He looked as thin as an old leaf, every bone sticking out. The blizzard had worn him down so far, there was almost nothing left.

Patrick and Mr. Teddy harnessed themselves to my sledge, and all three of us pulled together. Mr. Forde walked with Blossom, holding him up as they waded through the fresh drifts.

Blossom went in a wobbling, weaving way. He went as though every step would be his last. Then he stopped and refused to go farther, and it seemed he wanted to die right there. So Mr. Forde left him, and we all went on as the pony stood and sadly watched us go. But soon he came staggering along, lurching as though he had died but didn't know it. He managed mile after mile like that. Then his legs splayed out and he plopped on his belly.

It was a terrible thing to see. Blossom lay on the snow exactly like the old mare, his nose touching the surface. His eyes moved slowly. His breath was soft and wheezy.

I wished I could help him. I wanted to nudge him back to his feet, the way my mother had done for me on the day I was born. But I stood in my harness, and I couldn't move.

The men melted snow in their hands to let Blossom drink. They fed him oil cakes and sugar, or tried to. They covered him with blankets, put sacking on top, and kept rubbing, rubbing everywhere that the pony trembled.

There was no need for the knife. Blossom closed his eyes and slipped away.

He lay at the very end of his tracks, with the marks of his hooves stretching away to the south, fainter and fainter, until they vanished in the wind-smoothed white of the Barrier.

I snorted quietly. Patrick looked over, then came to see me. He ducked his head under my nose and put his arm around my chest. "No worries, lad," he said. "We'll get you home, no fear."

There was another burial, another cairn. Then all together we pulled the sledge, three men and a pony working together. Every time we stopped, the men built the most enormous wall. They piled me high with every blanket and sack they could find. And they fed me Blucher's food, and Blossom's, as well as my own. They stuffed me full at every meal.

Day after day, we walked to the north, toward the lowest point of the sun. There, at midnight he sank below the horizon, only to rise again right after. I had watched his travels all my life and knew that he was heading for his wintering place, that he would soon be gone altogether.

It was a miserable time, but a wonderful time as well. I lived high on the hog with my extra rations, and I didn't feel like an old pony tagging along with the men. I felt like a companion, a friend.

When cracks began to appear in the ice, I knew we were getting close to the sea. The men went more carefully then, sometimes stomping on the snow to make sure it was solid.

We strolled along, everyone pleased to see Mount Erebus loom ahead of us, its plume of smoke like a welcoming flag. Patrick stroked my shoulder. "You've done it, James," he said. "You're home."

I thought so too. But with my next step, the snow broke apart underneath me. I dropped like a stone, right into a crevasse.

❄   ❄   ❄

It was an awful shock to have the ground fall away, to be suddenly standing on nothing. I felt my heart push up through my throat as I hurtled down. For just an instant, my eyes were level with Patrick's—and what a startled look I saw! Then he was above me and I was still falling.

I thought I was going to disappear inside the Barrier. But suddenly, with a thud, I came to a stop.

Luckily, my belly was a little bit wider than the crevasse, and I stuck in the ice like a cork.

The men watched me squirm and kick. My hooves were dangling underneath me, above a frightening chasm that might have been bottomless for all I could see. The men looked awfully surprised at first, but soon they started laughing.

"It's all that high living," said Mr. Teddy. "It's saved your life, James Pigg."

Mr. Forde got a long rope from the sledge. They tied it around me and pulled together. They rolled me out onto the snow, and I squirmed like a beetle until I managed to get myself up. The men kept laughing, but there was nothing mean or cruel about it. I *was* a bit roly-poly.

When he saw that I was safe, Patrick walked right to the edge of the crevasse. He bent down and peered into it. "It's very blue," he said, smiling. "Deep and dark."

I went over to see for myself. I stood right beside Patrick, hung my head like him, and together we stared straight down into the darkness. We stared and we stared, then I turned my head and looked at my friend.

Mr. Forde and Mr. Teddy found this enormously funny. I didn't know why. They put their hands on their thighs and bent forward, laughing all over again. Patrick grinned at me in the way that made me feel warm inside. "That was a near shave for you, James Pigg," he said.

Far to the west, at his hut on the Barrier, Amundsen is doing some housekeeping between his journeys to the depots. He takes time to make sure that his dogs will survive the winter in comfort.

From the beginning, he has provided tents for the dogs. Until now, they've been sitting on the surface, but that won't do when temperatures fall to forty and fifty and sixty below. So he sinks the floor of each tent six feet into the Barrier, chopping the ice with axes. Then he drives twelve posts into the floor, spaced evenly along the wall. One dog will be tethered to each post. Otherwise, they would kill each other before spring.

With that job done, Amundsen loads seven sledges and sets off again to the south. In two weeks, he'll travel beyond his last depot, all the way to 82 degrees south, but his dogs will be worn out. "This is my only dark memory of my stay in the South," he writes later, "the over-taxing of these fine animals. I had asked more of them than they were capable of doing. My consolation is that I did not spare myself either."

❄   ❄   ❄

Scott is worried about some of his men and how they will fare in the spring. Oates's nose seems always on the point of frostbite; Meares has trouble with his feet. Both Cherry-Garrard and Scott himself have been nipped by frostbite on the cheeks. Bowers, who wears nothing on his head but a felt hat, never seems to feel the cold. But Scott sees that his ears have turned white.

On February 18, Scott hurries ahead to meet Teddy Evans and the others he had sent back with the crocks. He goes by dogsled and is amazed by the speed and endurance of the dogs. From morning to lunch, they take him seventeen miles.

"The way in which they keep up a steady jog trot for hour after hour is wonderful," he writes. "Their legs seem steel springs, fatigue unknown—for at the end of a tiring march any unusual incident will arouse them to full vigour."

CHAPTER SIX

AT Safety Camp we rested. It was a lovely place, cold and quiet, with the men's tent like a tiny gray mountain on the plain of ice. We could see Mount Erebus smoldering away to the west, and the glaciers oozing out onto the Barrier. A glacier moved so slowly that I imagined it saw everything else go by in a blur, the sun and moon dashing round and round the world like an eagle chasing a sparrow.

We expected a long wait for the others to catch up, but after just a day or two, we were surprised by the sound of dogs approaching.

All of us turned toward the distant yapping. We saw tiny black specks far off to the south, rising over the crests of the snow waves. There and gone, that's how they came: a little bigger, a little louder, every time they reappeared.

Two teams of dogs were running side by side, as though racing each other. The men ran beside the sledges, sometimes holding on with one hand. They stumbled and rose and ran on again. I saw Captain Scott and Mr. Meares at one of the sleds. At the other was young Gran, and then Cherry with his glass eyes on his nose. That made everything seem so fine. I was always happy when I saw Cherry.

Men and dogs, they flew toward us, weaving around the crests of snow. We all watched them come. I peered above my snow wall. Mr. Forde looked out from the tent where he was cooking. Mr. Teddy and Patrick raised their heads from the overturned sledge, where they were sharpening the metal edges of the runners.

The dog Osman was leading a team. I watched him leap at his harness, and all the others leap behind him. Every dog in every team was silent now, exhausted by their travel. We could hear them panting as their paws pattered along.

The dog Osman veered around the end of a ridge and galloped across the flat space behind it. The others followed him two by two, leaning into the turn. The second team fell back a bit, and someone yelled at them in Russian, telling them to hurry.

I felt the old twinge inside me. I remembered men *screaming* those words, and I saw—in my mind—a red-faced Russian raising a whip, his eyes full of fury.

The memory was more real than the dogs and the sled and the pale streaks of the clouds. I winced from the whip, closing my eyes as I waited for the sting. So I didn't see the dogs plummet through the snow.

It was the sound that brought me out of my memory, a frantic noise of dogs and men. I saw the dog Osman standing alone in the snow, leaning forward with his feet planted firmly, as though he was pulling a thousand pounds but not moving an inch. Behind him was a gaping hole, a crevasse so wide and deep that every dog except for Osman had vanished inside it. On the other side sat the sledge, tilted at the very lip of the crevasse. Captain Scott and Mr. Meares had leapt clear, but already they were on their feet and hurrying back.

All around the sledge, the snow was cracked and crumbling. The men wrestled it sideways and anchored it firmly where the snow was solid. The traces stretched taut in front of it, into the crevasse and up again on the other side, where the dog Osman was holding the weight of his whole team. He was strangling in his harness, breathing in painful rasps. But he held his ground, and as much as I hated that dog, I had to admit he looked heroic.

A hideous howling came up from the ice. Mr. Teddy and Mr. Forde ran out to help. Patrick untied me from my picket and hurried me around the wall. "They'll be needing you now, James Pigg," he said.

I went at a trot as he ran beside me.

It was a bridge of snow that had caved in, a cover for the crevasse. If the sledge had gone another foot or two, if it had weighed another pound, it would have crashed through the snow along with the dogs, taking Captain Scott with it, down and down through the Barrier.

Patrick led me in beside the dog Osman. He could tell I was scared to go near that beast, and he kept talking to me calmly. "Easy, lad. It's all right," he said. But the smell of the dog made me want to run away.

Cherry and Gran had turned their team around and stopped their sledge. They ran across the snow toward Captain Scott.

Patrick took me right to the edge. I looked straight down into the crevasse. It was much wider and deeper than the one that had nearly swallowed me. I could see a hundred feet down, but not all the way to the bottom. The ice was pale blue at the top, growing darker and darker until everything faded away.

Sixty feet down, part of the bridge had jammed between the sides of the crevasse to make a narrow shelf. Two of the dogs lay there, on their sides, absolutely still. The rest dangled from their harnesses, some upside down, some sideways, all howling in terror. Two were swinging back and forth, back and forth, like enormous spiders at the ends of their threads. And every time they swung together, each snarled and snapped, trying to grab the other by the throat.

Then Patrick turned me around and led me up beside the dog Osman. The smell of that dog put into my mind an image of Weary Willy fighting off the team. I was so scared that I shied away, and if not for Patrick, I might have fallen back right into the crevasse. But he kept his hold on my halter and stood between me and the dog. As we went past, the dog Osman raised its head and looked at me. For the first time, I stared straight into a dog's eyes. I expected a black look of evil, but all I saw was fear and pleading. The dog couldn't hold on for much longer. Already it trembled with the effort of holding the other dogs, and the weight was slowly dragging it back toward the crevasse. A long rut was scraped in the snow, carved with the deep slashes of the dog's claws.

I was not wearing my collar, not rigged for a harness. Cherry brought a rope and put a loop around my shoulders. He cinched me up to the dog harness. Then Patrick stepped me forward, and the weight the dog was holding came onto me instead.

I leaned into it. My hooves slipped, nearly dragging me down. But I planted them solidly and heaved on the rope. I took all the weight on my shoulders. Then Cherry whip-ped out his knife and freed the dog Osman. The dog bounded forward, then stopped and turned around.

I hadn't imagined us changing places, with me tethered and the dog standing free. Its mouth was open, its tongue hanging out, a pink slather slithering between enormous fangs, in and out over gums as black as coal.

The dog could have attacked. It could have torn my throat wide open before anyone could help.

But it didn't. It stood facing me squarely, then bowed down on the snow with its front legs straight. It touched its chin to the ground. A feeling passed between us—a feeling of thanks and understanding. Then Gran came up beside the dog, grabbed a fistful of fur and neck, and hauled the creature away.

Behind me, on the other side of the crevasse, the men had freed the sledge and pushed it over the chasm to make a bridge. They worked there, hoisting the dogs two by two. With my head swung sideways I watched the dogs thrashing up to the surface, rolling out onto the snow. My load grew lighter and lighter, until there was nothing there at all.

Then Mr. Scott went down into the crevasse. There were

still the two dogs on the shelf, and he was too kindly to leave them. So he tied himself to the rope and stepped backward over the edge.

"Lower away!" he shouted. "Smartly now." The Barrier swallowed him up. The rope hissed through the snow, and the men leaned over the edge, watching.

"Easy now!" His voice echoed in the crevasse. He went very slowly for the last bit, so his weight wouldn't break the ledge. "Right, I've got them," he shouted up at us. And a moment later, "Good gracious, they're both asleep!"

Captain Scott sent up the dogs, then up he came himself. Before he even reached the surface, a big battle broke out among the dogs, one team against the other. The men had to leave the captain dangling while they sorted it out. It was a long time before everyone stood on the surface again.

❄   ❄   ❄

When Captain Scott heard about Blucher and Blossom, all the air came out of him in a great sigh, as though someone had squashed him like a puffball. He looked to the south, over the horizon.

"I should have sent them back sooner," he said.

"It wouldn't have made much difference, I think," said Mr. Teddy. "They were the worst of the crocks."

Captain Scott shook his head. "Such a waste." His voice was so quiet that he might have been speaking to himself. "Such a dreadful waste."

He sounded very sorry and sad. I wished I could tell him

that he was wrong, that it was not a waste. But I wasn't sure if Blossom and Blucher would have wanted me to do that.

Captain Scott stayed just long enough to eat a meal. He was eager to reach the hut, to see if there was news from his ship. As he passed on his way to the sledge, he stopped to give me a bit of biscuit from his pocket.

"Thank goodness James Pigg is all right," he said.

A moment later he was gone. The two teams of dogs ran side by side, bounding over the Barrier in a flurry of snow. We all watched until we couldn't see them anymore, then settled back to our waiting.

❄ ❄ ❄

I had always liked to see winter settling in. It meant an end to the flies and the heat. It slowed down the wolves; it put the bears into hiding. It made everything so soft and still.

But now I felt scared instead of happy. There was no shelter or stable out on the Barrier, no grass beneath the snow. The sun was going away, the darkness coming quickly. And I saw that winter would be long and hard.

We passed the time by hauling more supplies to Corner Camp. We trekked there and back and were heading north when a blizzard overtook us. It was the worst we'd seen. We made a camp on the Barrier, but the tents were soon covered in mounds of snow. Behind my wall, I stood in white slush as deep as my belly.

When the weather cleared, the men dug us out slowly. They kept glancing toward the south, talking of Mr. Oates and

Birdie Bowers and all the others, wondering how they'd coped with the blizzard. They were trying to laugh but sounded worried.

No one wanted to say that he'd given up hope. But as soon as the surface hardened again, we packed up and moved along. My sledge was nearly empty, quite easy to pull once I got it moving. But I stopped often to watch for Uncle Bill and the ponies, though it meant pulling hard for a while to get moving again. A white fog fell thickly on the Barrier, but still I kept looking back, though I never saw anything but whiteness behind me. In the end, I heard the men and ponies long before I saw them. The crunch of hooves and boots came out of the mist.

Patrick didn't understand why I stopped again so suddenly. "What's the matter, lad?" he asked.

I twitched my ears, trying to hear where the sounds were coming from. There was a grinding from the sledges behind us now, and a soft thump as a pony's crossbar touched the snow. I raised my head; I twitched my ears.

Patrick shuffled sideways as I turned in the harness. Then, together, we peered into the fog. Somewhere in the mist, a pony snorted and a man spoke softly.

Patrick put his hands to his mouth and shouted, "Hello, the party." A moment later, someone shouted back: "Hello yourself."

Uncle Bill was first to appear from the fog, plodding along in the lead. Little Birdie Bowers took shape at his side, and the others came after him, stepping out of the white and the gray. All covered with frost, they looked like creatures made of ice.

Guts was next. Then Punch, then Nobby close behind him. They seemed thin and cold and tired. They barely raised their heads to look at me, and I felt a bit ashamed to be standing there and watching them. Then they passed by me and disappeared into the fog again, trekking along to the north, heading for the winter station. I watched until Nobby had faded away, then waited for Weary Willy.

A long time went by. In the swirls of white, I saw things that weren't there: a fox, a bird, a butterfly. Patrick grew tired of waiting. He wanted to turn me around and follow the others. But when he tugged on my halter, I held my ground.

Patrick knew me well enough then to know what I was thinking. "I'm sure they'll be along," he said. "No sense in standing here, lad. We'll hear the story from Birdie."

But I still didn't move. I listened so carefully that I heard the thumpa-thump of Patrick's heart through his bones and his skin and his clothes. Then I heard the ring of a hoof on a patch of ice. I snorted, and Weary Willy answered with the smallest little breath.

He came out of the fog like a sack of bones, his skin hanging down from his belly. His eyes were a sickly yellow, his nostrils limp and fluttering.

I had seen starving ponies—plenty of them—but few as bad as Weary. He might have been on his way to the slaughtering house, plodding along on the last hundred yards of his life. Mr. Oates on his right side, young Gran on his left, were trying to help him along. But old Weary barely had the strength to lift his hooves, and didn't care where he placed them. So he stumbled and lurched on the trail. He didn't even turn his head to look at me.

We fell into line behind them, Patrick and I, Mr. Forde and Mr. Teddy. I was glad that everyone was together again, all of us heading north to our winter place.

But I worried about Weary. With his every step, I thought he'd fall. He struggled on, though, and was rewarded with kindness when we straggled into Safety Camp. Gran built him a very nice wall, then put extra sacks on his back. But the cold that came with the darkness was almost too much for the old pony. I listened to him breathing, a wheeze and a whistle that faded away until I thought each breath was his last.

When the sun came up, he was still there, though ragged and limp. And Mr. Oates was still at his side.

Gran brought hot mash, and that seemed to perk up poor Weary. If he could go another few miles, he'd reach the stable. He'd be warm and sheltered there. He could stuff himself with oil cakes and forage.

It was a good day for marching, clear and cold. But Weary couldn't walk, and Mr. Oates wouldn't leave him behind. So everyone stayed, with the wind tearing at the tents, whipping flurries over the pony walls.

❄   ❄   ❄

He was just a few miles from the stable, just a couple of days from a straw bed and a hot stove. He must have known it himself. But, just as surely, I knew that he would never make it, that he would die out there on the Barrier.

The men would build another lonely cairn, to mark the grave of another pony. They would erect a spike of snow in a world of snow, and it scared me to think of Weary Willy lying in the ice as it carried him slowly to the sea. It would be years and years and years before he reached it, the Barrier moved so slowly. But one day he would tumble out from the edge, frozen and stiff, and the killer whales would tear away his legs. I wondered: Would anyone be there to see him? Would they wonder who he was, and *why* he was, and could they ever guess in a thousand years how far he'd come to get there?

It was a sad day. And it was a sad night that followed, with Weary shivering away, breathing his rasping breaths.

I remembered how stubborn and lazy he'd been. I remembered him fighting the dogs and kicking his wall. But I didn't want to think about that, so I remembered Jehu instead, until a terrible fear came over me that I would never see *him* again, either. Then I tried to think of happy times in my life from before I knew the Englishmen. But I had to go all the way back to my days running free in the forest, to the time when I had never heard of people.

When the morning came, I tried not to look at Weary. I watched the tents instead, and finally Patrick came out to feed me an oil cake. As I ate the first half, he rubbed the coldness out of my legs. "You'll be glad to get into your stable, won't you, James Pigg?" he said. "Any day now."

He rubbed my shoulders and my neck. He fed me the rest of the oil cake, then peered across the Barrier with his eyes squinted. "Now, who's that coming this way in such a dreadful hurry?" he asked.

The men came on skis, in long fast strides, driving with their ski poles, pumping with their arms.

Everyone piled out of their tents. We watched the little figures growing larger. The skis flashed sunlight, kicking up sparkles of snow.

"It's Captain Scott," said Mr. Oates.

"Yes," said Birdie Bowers, squinting. "And Thomas Crean, I think."

He was right. The two men had dashed from the hut at the lonely place and didn't waste any time by chatting. "Get the ponies moving," shouted Captain Scott before he'd even joined us. "The ice is going out."

Mr. Oates looked alarmed. Birdie Bowers stared up at him with the same frightened look. Patrick reached out and touched my shoulder. "Steady, James," he said, as though to steady himself.

I remembered our trek around the glacier, where Guts had fallen through a hole to the sea. The ice had been dangerous then, the floes already breaking apart. If we couldn't get back across, and back around the glacier, we'd be stuck on the Barrier when winter came, sure to freeze to death.

"What about Weary Willy?" asked Mr. Oates.

Captain Scott looked toward the poor old pony. Weary stood shivering behind the wall, his nose nearly touching the ground. "Titus, there isn't much time," he said.

"I can't leave him behind." Mr. Oates tightened his wind helmet. "I shall stay."

He turned and walked away. Captain Scott watched him for a moment, then sighed. "Wait," he said. "I'll stay with you." He bent down to free his feet from the bindings of his skis.

The rest of us left in a terrible hurry. Tents and camping gear were thrown in a muddle onto the sledges. I and the other ponies were harnessed, and we set off toward the sea. Mr. Crean came with us, leaving his skis for Mr. Oates. My last sight of old Weary was sad but lovely: the pony shivering in his tattered green blanket; a man on each side of him rubbing and petting; the haunting hugeness of the Barrier stretching forever behind them. Then Patrick turned my head and we plodded along in the line.

In the lead were Uncle Bill and Birdie Bowers. At the back were me and Patrick. When we reached the edge of the Barrier, we were spread in a straggly line high above the sea.

Below us, the floating ice was streaked with blue, colored by sea and sky. Through gaps between the floes swam killer whales and leopard seals, while penguins stood, like little specks, scattered all around. The tracks of the dogsleds wove across the ice, broken already by the shifting floes.

A black mist was gathering high above us. It fell quickly, like a thing swooping upon us, and it blotted out the sun as we started down a snowy slope toward the ice. It settled on the land, thick as night, with a feeling of gloom and despair.

Far ahead, Uncle Bill was swallowed by the blackness. I watched for the marks of his big hooves in the snow, and knew he was all right as long as I could see them. Patrick sang to me softly, so I wasn't afraid.

For once my sledge moved easily. It moved *too* easily on the slope; it nearly ran me over. Patrick had to walk behind and hold it back as I trotted down through the black fog.

At the bottom, I found Uncle Bill and Guts and Nobby and Punch. They were out of breath, their ribs heaving. We all gathered close together and set off as one, across the floating ice.

Nearly right away, the immense cliff of the Barrier vanished behind us. Birdie Bowers led the way by his compass, as though through a tunnel in the mist. I heard the curious sounds of penguins, the booming breaths of killer whales, the scary creaks and cracks of the ice. Patrick had stopped singing. He tightened his fist in my halter, his knuckles pressing more tightly on my cheek.

The men were anxious to get off the ice. It was thick but not solid. I sometimes felt it shifting underneath me, though the men didn't seem to notice. As the sledges dragged along, water bubbled up through thin little cracks that split the surface into giant shards.

I snorted and shook my head, hoping the men would see that the ice wasn't safe. The farther we went, the more I worried. I saw more cracks, wider cracks, and a place where I was sure a pony could fall through. But it was a long time before Birdie Bowers stopped Uncle Bill and looked around with a worried expression.

"I don't like the look of this ice," he said.

"What's wrong with it?" asked Mr. Crean.

"I think it's moving." Birdie Bowers stamped a foot, as though that tiny weight could shift the ice. "How much farther to the hut, do you think?"

No one could say for sure. We couldn't see fifty feet in any direction, and Birdie's compass—though a wizard at finding direction—didn't have a clue about distance.

"I think we should turn back," said Birdie. "Make for the

harder ice along the shore. We can give the ponies a rest and wait for the fog to lift."

The ice creaked just then. It sounded like a great tree swaying in the wind. But out there in the fog, on top of the sea, it was a heart-stopping sound.

Suddenly, every man agreed with Birdie. We wheeled the sledges around and started back along our trail.

"Look at this. Oh, look at this," said Birdie. Cracks that had been a hair's thickness when we crossed them were wide enough that a man could slip his thumb inside them. Cherry peered through his glass eyes, but they didn't let him see any farther through the fog.

We all hurried along, trying to reach solid ice before dark.

It was Nobby who set the pace. He pulled his sledge forward step by step, with growing pauses between them. His breath wheezed and rasped. Even with a man helping him, poor Nobby could not go faster than a snail.

We didn't make it to the shore. We stopped at the first solid-looking bit of ice, and Birdie had a little walk around, in and out of the fog's black edge. "It isn't great," he said, with an awful worry. "But I think it might do."

The men built their camp. They spaced the sledges apart, set up our picket line, and piled up crumbly walls of snow. Soon their little stoves were hissing away, and I smelled our mash growing hot and bubbly.

When the sun went down, it brought the darkest night of all my life. I could not see my own hind hooves. I couldn't see the snow below my head, and I had a terrible thought that I was floating away in the fog. I imagined myself a thousand feet up, blowing south with the wind, an invisible sea below me. Frightened, I stamped my feet; I touched my nose to the ground, to make sure that it was still there.

Again, I couldn't sleep. I watched the fog break up hours later, when the moon came out and pushed it away. Then the southern lights flashed blue and green across the sky, and they filled my mind with memories of the northern forests. I remembered running under *northern* lights that were just the same, running at a full gallop with the cold wind in my lungs, my mane blowing back, running just for the sake of running.

It was the last time I had ever run like that, free and fearless. It was before the men had come and taken me. I'd been weighted down ever since by logs and carts and sledges.

The thought made me terribly sad. I looked toward the tents and found it comforting to see them, dark and shadowy against the shining lights.

I could see the other ponies behind their walls, Guts not far away at all, Uncle Bill—asleep, it seemed—his head swaying very slowly. I imagined they were all thinking, like me, of times long past.

The sun came up again, small and meek. It still stretched its long shadows over the ice, but it had lost a great deal of the fierceness and heat it had shown just weeks before. I imagined it was fading away before its winter hibernation.

As the day brightened, I was surprised to see great patches of empty sea all around us. The floe was breaking up. Our own bit of ice was fractured by the narrow sort of cracks that had startled Birdie Bowers. There was one between my feet, another right beside me. A thicker one, wide as a plank, zigzagged under Guts and passed below his wall.

I snorted loudly, hoping the men would come out of their tents.

Then, with an almighty bang, the ice split along the zigzagging line. That crack, in an instant, was wider than a pony, and I was nearly thrown to the ice by the movement of the floe. When I looked at Guts, he was gone.

His wall stood cleaved in two. His tether line hung broken. It was as though an invisible giant had swung a giant axe and opened the ice underneath the pony. The edges of the wall were still crumbling, the blocks toppling into black water. But of Guts, not a hair was showing.

From the tent came a shout. "The ponies!" cried Birdie Bowers. "They're helping themselves to the oats."

He thought what he'd heard was a sledge overturning, and he was out of the tent in a flash. He didn't bother with his boots but came running out in his socks and nearly stepped right through the crack, nearly right off the ice and into the sea. But he caught himself at the edge. He looked left and right, his face drawn into wrinkles and ridges.

"The ice!" he shouted now. "Cherry! Crean! We're floating out to sea!"

Little Birdie Bowers stepped well back from the gap. He was on one side of it, and I was on the other. I looked up and down, and saw that I was all alone on a little island of ice.

I whinnied for help. I tried to pull myself free from the tether line. But all I did was tug on the sledge behind me, where the line was anchored on my own lonely little island.

115

Birdie Bowers gaped at me. So did Uncle Bill, his lips pulled back from his teeth.

The ice shifted. The gap closed with a grinding sort of crunch, then slowly began to open again.

On the other side, Birdie Bowers rubbed his hands together. Then he squared his feet, bent forward, and ran straight toward the widening gap. His little feet pattered on the snow. At the edge, he launched himself forward and flew above the water like a puppet flung through the air. He tumbled onto my island, leapt to his feet, and hurried to untie me. But the knots were stiff, the rope frozen.

He attacked them with his teeth. The ice moved again, nearly knocking Birdie from his feet. He gave up on the rope and tugged instead on the sledge.

He couldn't move it by himself. It weighed five hundred pounds and was frozen in its place. So I pulled as well. I backed across the ice, towing with my tether line. We moved the sledge across the gap, and all of us were together again on the same broken bit of ice. Or all except Guts, who was gone forever without a sound.

And with another bang, our one big island split in two.

❄   ❄   ❄

The men struck their tents. They threw them on the sledges. Birdie Bowers took just enough time to sit down and put on his boots.

"We have been in a few tight places," he said. "But this is about the limit."

The sledges were loaded. I and the other ponies were harnessed. We were ready to move, but it wasn't clear at all which way we should go.

We could see land ahead; the snowy slope to the Barrier was behind us. To our right was the glacier, impossible to climb, and on our left were endless floes of ice, all drifting out to sea. Our little islands were going along with them.

Captain Scott was on the Barrier, the rest of our people at the wintering place. The ice seemed thickest behind us, so we headed back. We fled for the slope that would lead us up to the Barrier.

"Keep together!" shouted Birdie.

He led us on, steering Uncle Bill around splits and cracks. But when we came to the first wide gap, the big pony wouldn't cross it. He shied away from the water, tossing his head so violently that he nearly pulled the little man off his feet.

The crack was less than two feet wide. For Uncle Bill, it was just a step. But he wouldn't do it, no matter how Birdie pulled at his tether. The men took off our harnesses and freed us from the sledges, but even then, Uncle Bill wouldn't cross the gap. I didn't blame him for that; it was scary to look at the black water and think how deep and cold it was, to think of what lived inside and might be waiting right there below the ice. I had seen the killer whales hunting, and I was terrified that one would come bursting through the gap at any moment. I didn't want to go *near* that place.

But Punch didn't mind. Punch was the sort of pony who didn't think about anything he couldn't see right in front of him. He had no imagination, and I sometimes thought he was lucky for that. Cherry led him away, then turned him back in a circle, speeding him up until he jogged beside a trotting pony. Together they ran toward the gap, and together they crossed it. The ice shook as Punch pounded along.

I went next. Patrick held me firmly and told me not to worry. "It's like crossing a puddle, is all," he said.

I didn't look down. But I couldn't help seeing the black streak below me. I imagined it was just a puddle on springtime snow and that the worst I could do was wet my foot if I missed a step. Patrick pulled. He stepped across the gap.

I closed my eyes and followed him. I had followed that man for so far that it was easy.

Nobby came next, then Uncle Bill tried again. He still snorted and pranced, big puffs of breath jetting from his nostrils. But it was either cross the water or stay by himself on a crumbling island. So he made up his mind and went over with a mighty leap, as though crossing a great canyon. Then he looked so pleased with himself, so proud, that Birdie Bowers gave him a piece of biscuit.

The men left us on our new bit of ice and brought the sledges across. Then we moved along to the next gap. Punch went straight across, but the gap widened even as he crossed it. Patrick held me back until the floes came closer again. Then I and Nobby and Uncle Bill went across together.

From gap to gap we moved along, from island to island. The ponies went first, then the men hurried back for the sledges. We headed for a sloping island that made a ramp to the Barrier, where the cliff was less than twenty feet high. But for every yard we gained, the floe took us a foot in the other direction.

I wasn't afraid. Neither were Punch and Uncle Bill. We trusted the men, and waited for them at every crossing. I felt bad that they pulled the sledges, heaving in the harnesses until they were red and panting.

At last we had only two gaps to cross to reach the sloping island. But as we waited for the first to close, the killer whales arrived.

Their black fins sliced up through the water. Their breaths puffed up in steamy spouts. One held up its head and stared at us, and we saw its wicked rows of teeth gleaming like the snow.

Back and forth they swam in front of us. I heard their voices in the water; I felt them through the ice. Others came from all around, gathering in the gaps.

The floes were shifting. When they jammed together, we went across—all at once—in a line like a cavalry charge. The men rushed back for the sledges and we moved on to the last gap. So did the whales.

Again we waited for our chance, and again we got across. We climbed the slope toward the Barrier, Birdie Bowers so happy now that he whistled as we walked.

But at the top, there was a terrible disappointment. The ramp did not reach all the way to the Barrier. There was a gulf of water forty feet across, and it stretched for miles on either side.

The sea swell rolled through it, bouncing off the Barrier, bouncing off the ice, churning that gulf into wild white water. Huge chunks of ice tossed and tumbled, and the whales swam everywhere, their breaths a terrific roar.

Birdie Bowers looked beaten. I could feel his despair as he looked at that stretch of water. Our only safety was on the other side, but crossing was impossible.

The men got out their stoves. They brewed tea for themselves, and hot mash for the rest of us, then sat on a sledge, all in a row. They didn't talk, but I could sense the worry shared by the three of them.

In front of us, the killer whales swam back and forth. A seal barked from a distant floe, and a pair of penguins popped up to have a look at us. But the men looked only at the Barrier, watching for the wind.

If the wind picked up from the north or the west, we were safe. Our island would be blown across to the Barrier. But if the wind came instead from the south, we were finished. We would sail away on our icy little home, away from the winter station, away from our friends and our food. There was not a ship in all the land to save us.

And the wind almost always came from the south.

On the lip of the Barrier, little whirls of snow showed that the wind was already blowing up there. Cherry took off his glass eyes. He wiped them with his mitten, then put them on again, working their little arms under his wind helmet. Then he sat facing the west, and three times he slurped his tea. "You know," he said, "if a chap went off that way, he might find a place to get across to the hut. He could tell Captain Scott what's happened."

Birdie nodded. "I was thinking the same thing."

I believed they were right, but it was hard to tell. Far to the west, the ice did seem to butt up against the Barrier. But it might have been a trick that the ice was playing, the way it sometimes looked very close when it was really far away, or how it sometimes seemed to float upside down in the sky.

"It's worth a try," said Cherry. He bent down to tighten his boots for the long walk. But Birdie Bowers, looking very comfortable, said, "I say, it might be better if it's Crean who goes."

Mr. Crean suddenly sat up straight. Cherry blinked through his little glass eyes. "Why?" he asked.

"Well . . ." Birdie frowned and twitched. "Well, the chap has to *see*," he said with an awkward laugh. "You understand?"

Poor Cherry. I felt so sorry for him as he turned away. It wasn't his fault that he had to wear his eyes on his nose, hooked over his ears. He scraped a little rut into the snow with his boot. "Yes, of course," he said softly. "You're quite right."

So Mr. Crean headed off alone. We watched him work his way across the floes, standing in our little group—four ponies and two men.

Cherry hated to sit and do nothing. He got out a tent and began to set it up. "At least we'll have a marker," he said.

Birdie helped him. It was a job they could do very quickly, but one or the other was always looking away from the canvas and the poles, his head turned to the west. It was always Cherry who said, "Is that Crean I see now?" Or "Look; is that a group of men on the ice?" His glass eyes didn't work very well. Every time Cherry saw a man, Birdie said it was only a penguin.

When the tent was up, the men fed us again. They gave us our nose bags, with plenty of oats inside them. Punch and Nobby chewed away quite happily, but I kept watch for Mr. Crean. I didn't feel like eating until I knew he was safe. And at last he appeared on the Barrier, so far to the west that he was just a little dot with waving arms. He looked like a flea.

Cherry saw him too, and pointed. "Birdie?" he said. "Is that a man over there?"

Birdie sighed. He'd been asked to look at a hundred penguins. But now, as he turned and looked again, he laughed with delight. "Why, yes, it's Crean!" he cried. "Thank God one of us is out of the woods, anyhow."

The little flea waved its tiny arms again, then vanished onto the Barrier.

I knew he would find Captain Scott. I wasn't sure what *anyone* could do to help us, but I had no doubt that the captain would find some little trick. So again we waited. And the killer whales waited, standing up to watch us. Soon the skuas came, one by one, until a big black mass of them was sitting on the ice around us, hoping to get what was left when the whales had their feed. Everyone waited.

A big shard of ice came drifting in from the east. A sliver off an iceberg, or a fragment from the cliff, it was like an enormous broken tooth. It turned; it tilted. It drifted on.

When Cherry saw it, he started shouting. He started waving. "Over here!" he cried, half laughing. "Come on. This way."

The ice jammed to a floe to the east of us, then freed itself and drifted on again. Now Patrick called to it as well. They cheered as it came nearer. When one end touched our own little island, and the other end swung around and jarred up against the Barrier, Cherry and Birdie and Patrick all held their hands in the air and grinned at each other. They had a bridge now that would take them straight to shore. It was big enough for both of them, and maybe for a pony. But there were fifteen feet of cliff to climb on the other side. And only men could climb a cliff.

*   *   *

I didn't blame the men for being so happy. Their only chance for escape had appeared from nowhere, just when everything looked as bleak and dark as possible. It was as though their lives had been snatched away, then given back like a gift from the world.

They laughed as they set to work. They took everything off my sledge and put it on the other sledges. Then they used mine for a ladder, lowering one end to the bridge. They had just put it in place when a voice called across the strip of water. It was Captain Scott! He was standing at the edge of the Barrier, with Mr. Oates and Mr. Crean beside him.

Captain Scott shouted, "Come across. Hurry!"

Little Birdie Bowers answered, standing on his toes as he shouted, "What about the ponies?"

Captain Scott yelled back, "I don't give a damn about the ponies!"

It stung me to hear those words. At the same time, I knew why he said them. There was nothing else that he *could* say that would get Birdie to leave us behind and make his way to safety.

"It's you I want," shouted Captain Scott. "And I am going

to see you safe here up on the Barrier before I do anything else."

Birdie and Cherry started their way across. Birdie went first, down to the bridge of ice. Cherry followed. Then Patrick turned around to step backward onto the sledge. With his hands on the snow, his feet on the sledge, he raised his head for a moment and we found ourselves looking right into each other's eyes. I knew he had to go, but I didn't want it to happen.

I saw him swallow, a big lump bobbing in his throat. I tried to make it easier by turning away myself, though it was a hard thing to do. My eyes wanted to look again, to watch him go, but I wouldn't let them.

He called out to me. "So long, James Pigg," he said. "I promise I'll be back." And a moment later, he was gone, clambering down the sledge.

I saw him again, he and Birdie and Cherry together, lifting the sledge to the Barrier cliff. Killer whales snorted and roared, and the men scrambled up and over the top as Captain Scott and the others reached down to help them. Then they all moved away from the edge, and I couldn't see them anymore.

Whirls of snow came down from the lip of the Barrier. To the west a huge chunk of ice fell away, tumbling into the sea with a rumble and a great splash. Waves spread out through the gap, breaking against the bridge, nearly knocking it away.

A penguin leapt up to the ice. A killer whale cruised past it, puffing a breath that sparkled in the sun.

I thought of poor Guts, trapped suddenly under the ice in

that awful cold and darkness. I wondered if it had happened so quickly that he didn't really *know* it had happened. It would be good if that were true. In a way, I wished the ice would crack open right then and swallow *me*. I didn't want to drift around on a bit of ice until I starved to death.

Whatever was going to happen, it didn't matter to the skuas. They ruffled their wings and settled, hunched, in the snow. Their little black eyes were open, watching. Those birds, I thought, could sit and wait forever.

I felt rather sorry for myself just then. I had wanted to be such a help to Captain Scott and Mr. Oates and the others. I'd thought I would spend my last days with them, in one way or another. But now I was nothing but a worry to them, no use at all.

I was surprised when they came back to the edge of the Barrier. Uncle Bill noticed them first, and whinnied sadly for Birdie Bowers, who had cared for him as fondly as Patrick had cared for me. The big pony shifted on his feet. He dug at the snow with one hoof.

I supposed the men had come for one last look, as a way of saying good-bye. Mr. Oates had brought something long and thin that he rested on his shoulder. I thought it was probably a rifle. But when he swung it down from his shoulder, I saw that it was a shovel. Birdie came up behind him with another shovel, and together they started digging.

They pushed the blades into the surface. They pried with the handles and levered up chunks of snow that they tossed over the edge, down to the bridge. Then they did it again, cutting back from the edge. The snow splattered on the icy bridge with small explosions.

The men were making a ramp.

Patrick and Cherry started working beside them, using skis to dig in the snow. Mr. Crean used his hands, breaking off bits from the edge. Then Birdie scrambled down and across the bridge, bringing a shovel to start another ramp up to our island.

The work would take hours and hours, and the men raced against the wind. The gusts were stronger now, and shiny sprinkles whirled from the falling clods of snow. At any moment, a gale could come, and we'd go sailing out to sea.

Captain Scott was watching for that. He paced along the Barrier's edge, looking now to the south and now to the sea. Mr. Oates and the others were digging like fury. They had thrown off their heavy coats, their mittens and wind helmets. They bent and straightened, working the shovels without a moment's rest.

I felt the ice shift. The bridge jarred across the floe with a sound like teeth being ground together. Captain Scott shouted down to little Birdie, his voice shrill with urgency: "Bowers, come up!"

Birdie Bowers looked up. He wiped his forehead with his sleeve.

"Now!" screamed Captain Scott. "Come up, I say."

The bridge was breaking loose. It tipped to one side, spilling half of the snow that was piled on its top. Birdie grabbed his mittens and coat and raced for the Barrier.

He barely made it. He had to leap across a gap on the other side. Mr. Oates stretched out on his stomach, reaching out a hand to grab the little man. They hauled up the sledge, and an instant later, the bridge flopped on its side. A gap opened between its far end and the Barrier. There was two feet of water, then six feet of water, then twenty feet of water.

Uncle Bill hadn't taken his eyes off Birdie for a moment. Now he swayed as the ice shifted again. His tail swished sadly.

We had our blankets on. I was wearing two—my own and one that still smelled of Blossom. But I had never felt so cold as then.

The men went away, but not far. They must have pitched their tents as close as they dared to the edge, because there was always one of them—and often more—standing right at the edge. Patrick was there at the end of the day, as the clouds and the snow turned to the colors of fire.

Then everything faded away into blackness. The mountains disappeared; the Barrier vanished; the skuas eased out of sight. I wished the moon would come down through the clouds, but he didn't. The night was the loneliest I remembered, so cold that my breaths froze into icicles.

I could hear the whales and the birds, but I couldn't see them. Everything was invisible.

I moved close to Uncle Bill. He pressed against me, snorted, and began to nuzzle at my neck. Then Punch came and joined us, pushing up against my other side. Even squeezed between them, I was still cold, but it made the night less lonely.

In the morning, I saw that we had moved along in the darkness. Our little island was jammed in a mass of ice below the Barrier, at a place where the cliff had crumbled away. There was a slope from top to bottom.

I hoped to see Patrick looking down at me, but nobody was there. The killer whales had followed us. As I looked across the water, one lifted its head high from the surface and gazed back at me with its piggish eyes. And the skuas had moved nearer. The whole flock was gathered close by.

In the shadows below the cliff, something moved and caught my eye. I had to blink frost from my eyelashes and turn my head to see it properly. A little man was coming across the ice. He lurched and tipped, as though trying to keep his balance. I made a happy sound; I stomped my feet and shook my mane.

But it was only a penguin. I saw the white feathers at its front, its orange feet padding along. It hopped from one floe to another, then up onto our own small island. It waggled its stump of wings and made a funny chirping sound, then settled down, as though waiting to see what would happen.

The sun was climbing through the sky when I saw Patrick. He was still quite far away, but I knew for sure it was him. Soon I saw Mr. Oates and Captain Scott and Birdie Bowers too. They moved quickly along the edge of the Barrier, and then down the ramp to the ice.

Uncle Bill saw them. So did Nobby. Both turned in that direction, their ears twitching wildly. But Punch only blinked, blinded by the snow and glare.

Captain Scott and Patrick went off in different directions, looking for the best route across the ice. But Mr. Oates and Cherry and Birdie Bowers came straight to our island, hauling an empty sledge that they used to bridge across the widest gaps.

I could feel the hurry, the anxiousness inside them. Wispy

clouds were flying northward, and the wind would soon come down to the sea.

They chose Punch to go first. Birdie grabbed his tether rope and tugged him forward. Punch lurched down the slope toward the first gap, three feet wide. "Straight across," said Birdie, leading the pony faster.

Punch was cold and stiff, half blinded by the sun. But he trotted along beside the little man.

"Yes, yes," said Birdie, half running now. His short legs swished back and forth, and the skuas that sat by the water flew up in a great black horde.

Maybe it was the birds that frightened Punch. Something certainly did. At the very edge of the floe, he dug in his heels and Birdie had to leap across by himself, letting go of the rope.

The ice broke away, crumbling back from the edge. Punch cried out. He tipped forward headfirst and tumbled into the sea.

He surfaced again a moment later, such fear in his eyes that I looked away. I heard the killer whales talking. I saw their black fins veering toward us.

Punch tried to paw his hooves up to the ice, to pull himself to safety. He struggled and screamed. But the terrible cold of the water sapped his strength in a moment. He sagged down in the water, raised himself again, and then looked desperately around at the men.

Captain Scott and Patrick came running to help. All the men worked together, trying to keep hold of Punch. But he kicked and thrashed in the water, and there was no hope of pulling him out. In moments, the killer whales would be tearing at his legs, and it was the creaky feel of their voices that put such terror into poor old Punch.

Mr. Oates was holding a pick. It was Mr. Oates who had to do the awful thing.

I turned away. So did Patrick and Birdie Bowers. I heard the thud of the pick, and a grunt that might have come from either one, the pony or the man.

When I looked, Punch was gone, and Mr. Oates was standing there with the pick hanging from his hand. His back was toward me, his shoulders were hunched and his head hanging down.

Patrick came up and grabbed my rope. "Time to get you moving, James Pigg," he said. At the same time, Birdie took hold of Nobby and ran him toward the gap. The pony held back at first, then trundled along, faster and faster. But he veered aside at the last minute, nearly trampling Birdie.

"You'll have to show him how," said Patrick. He thumped my neck with the flat of his hand. He rubbed my nose. "Ready? Off we go," he told me.

I didn't dream of letting him down. When Patrick got me started, I trotted beside him. I sped up to a canter. We aimed right for the gap, where Punch's blood spotted the ice with speckles of red.

"Good lad! Good lad," cried Patrick, running beside me.

I wanted to lead the way to safety. But I wasn't a jumper. My legs were short, the water black and awful, full of killer whales and dead ponies. I wanted to jump. I didn't.

Like Nobby, I veered away. I turned toward Patrick, pushing him back until he stumbled and fell on the ice. I heard him groan as his shoulder hit the ground. I had to skitter my back legs to keep from running him down.

One of his mittens had been torn away. He got up and put it on again. "Well, James Pigg," he said. "Let's give that another try."

"No, that's enough," said Captain Scott. He looked angry but sounded sad. "It's no use. The ice will drift away before we get them all across. If the gap widens, we're all finished."

"We have to *try*," said Birdie Bowers.

Captain Scott shook his head. He looked at Mr. Oates, who was standing in silence with the pick in his hand. "Finish them now," he said. "They're lost at any rate."

If Captain Scott had been holding the pick instead of Mr. Oates, it might have been the end for me right there. It was Captain Scott who knew about ice, how it broke apart, how it rotted, how it drifted, and he knew there wasn't time to waste. He stepped toward Mr. Oates, reaching for the pick. "I'll do it, Titus," he said.

Birdie Bowers pretended not to hear. He took my rope. He turned me toward the gap. "Come on, Jimmy Pigg," he whispered. "It's up to you now."

I ran beside him. The edge of the ice was three feet away, then suddenly right below me. Birdie jumped, and so did I, pushing with my legs. I hurdled the gap. I bounded across it.

Patrick cheered. A great smile came to Mr. Oates. He was standing next to Uncle Bill, so he took the pony's tether and raced him to the water.

Uncle Bill was big and heavy. Once he was moving, he was hard to stop. He went straight for the gap, but he didn't jump. It was as though he didn't see it right in front of him. He just blundered to the edge of the floe—and right across to the next one. When he stood beside me, he seemed surprised to be there.

Old Nobby came easily then, anxious to stay with the leader. Captain Scott hurried us on, and from floe to floe we moved toward the slope. Most of the jumps were easy, the gaps just a foot or two wide, and we crossed steadily from island to island, and came at last to the final floe. I was the first to reach it, bounding across. But it was a very narrow island, and a big pool of open water was suddenly right in front of me.

Patrick veered me off to the left and straight across another gap. I jumped without thinking. And I sighed to see that I was safe, standing on solid ice at the foot of the Barrier.

Nobby came behind me. I watched him leap the first gap, swing to the left, jump again to safety.

Uncle Bill was already huffing across the snow, trying to catch up. He crossed the first gap and turned left, with Birdie nudging him.

Just as he started the second jump—in the moment he timed his leap—a dozen killer whales surfaced in the pool. They came in a surge of water, with their shocking breaths as loud as gunshots. Their heads towered up, their piggy eyes staring.

Uncle Bill tried to twist away from them. He was half in the air as he turned, and he landed just half on the ice. His back legs splashed into the sea, and he hung from the foot of the Barrier with his head and shoulders high above the surface. His eyes swiveled around as he looked in terror for the whales.

At one time, Uncle Bill might have pulled himself easily onto the ice. But now he was old and cold and hungry. Birdie grabbed his mane. Someone else took hold of his halter. But they couldn't pull him up.

"Leave him," said Captain Scott. "Bowers, please!"

He was right. All around the floundering pony, where the men huddled to help him, the ice was cracked and shattered. They might end up in the sea at any moment, but Birdie Bowers wouldn't give up. "I can't leave him to be eaten alive by those whales," he said.

The pick was lying on the ice. Both he and Mr. Oates looked at it. There was a wretched expression on Mr. Oates's face. "I shall be sick if I have to kill another horse as I did the last," he said.

"Give me the pick," said Birdie. "He's my horse."

Mr. Oates fetched the pick. It might have weighed a thousand pounds, the way he dragged it behind him. He let it fall on the ice as he bent down and pointed out a spot on Uncle Bill's forehead. Then he walked away with his head hunched down, as though trying to cover his ears with his shoulders.

For Uncle Bill, there was one last pet and a whispered good-bye. Then Birdie swung the pick, and very quickly it was over.

We went along the ice and up to the Barrier. Nobody looked back at the sea, at the scattered floes we'd crossed. We just walked in a stunned sort of silence, with Birdie carrying the halter that Uncle Bill had worn for so long. He was so sad that he *smelled* of sadness.

For me, it was awful to lose Uncle Bill. A pony without a leader was a lonely and wandering soul. I suddenly wanted to get to the stable as quickly as possible. I had to see Hacken-schmidt, my old silvery stallion from so long ago. I believed he'd be better now, tamed at last by the Englishmen all around him. I couldn't bear to think of anything else, not after the things I had seen.

※　　※　　※

It was nearly the end of our first season. The days were ever shorter, and the sun was setting as we tramped around the edge of Mount Erebus. Eight ponies had gone out to lay depots, and only two came back.

I was in the lead. Me and Patrick. Sore and tired, I was looking forward to stopping, to a long winter's rest in the sta-ble. With one more hill to cross, I smelled the straw. It seemed the most beautiful, wonderful odor in the world. And I hurried then. At the crest of the hill, I whinnied to let Hackenschmidt know I was coming.

He didn't answer. But Jehu did. That surprised me a bit, and pleased me a whole lot more. I leaned forward and hur-ried, over the crest and down to the winter station.

It was all suddenly spread out below me. The wooden hut at the side of the sea, the stable against it, now roofed and complete. Little sheds here and there. Men busy at strange tasks. A pony racing wildly over the snow with a rider on its back. And little Jehu looking up at me, wriggling happily to see me arrive.

But where was Hackenschmidt? I called out again. Still, he didn't answer.

Some of the men looked up. They saw Patrick and

me coming over the rise, then Mr. Crean with Nobby, then Captain Scott and Mr. Oates all harnessed to the sledge, pulling it along. The men below waved, then started running up the slope.

I had never arrived at a place full of men and gotten a welcome like that. I was greeted as warmly as anyone, the men calling out—"Hello, Patrick." "Hello, Titus." "Hello, Jimmy Pigg!"—as though all of us were equal.

Then they saw that there were no more ponies behind us. And all the happiness turned to a solemn sort of wonder. Birdie Bowers still carried his pony's halter; he had scarcely put it down in two or three days. He tried to tell what had happened but couldn't finish speaking. So others told the story as we trekked down toward the hut, wading now through softer snow.

"And what of Hackenschmidt?" asked Mr. Oates at last. "Still as mean as ever, is he?"

"Not quite," said one of the men who'd stayed behind.

Mr. Oates laughed. "You don't mean he's improved?"

"*Much* improved," said the fellow. "He's dead."

It was shocking news, and I hated that the man was happy to tell it. I hated that others laughed to hear it. Only Mr. Oates seemed the least bit sad. "What happened?" he asked.

The fellow shrugged, as though it didn't really matter how the pony had died.

"When?" asked Mr. Oates.

"Weeks ago. Not long after you left, I'd say."

Patrick reached out and patted my neck. I pushed against him, wanting to feel the same comfort from his touch that I'd found in my mother's gentle nuzzling. It made me feel terrible inside to think that the silvery stallion had been dead a long time. I'd wanted so badly to see him again.

"One day, he stopped eating," said the fellow. "He didn't eat or drink; he didn't want to leave the stable. He just lay down and died."

Mr. Oates looked worried. "Was it colic?" he said. "Was it glanders?"

"No," said the other. "The biologist couldn't explain it. If you ask me, it was cussedness. He'd do anything to avoid his work."

In his hut, with his work done, Amundsen greets winter with pleasure. Looking out at the Barrier through his kitchen window gives
him a feeling of comfort and well-being.

He sets up a nursery for his pregnant dogs and lets the others
run loose through the day. Their manners, he says, have improved
and they come back on their own to be fed, each heading to its own
post in its own tent, where it is fastened up for the night. Big battles are rare these days.

He rations time spent with the gramophone, afraid his men will
grow tired of it. But every evening, there's a glass of toddy and a
cigar, and no one tires of that.

When the sun disappears and the temperatures fall, his men dig
tunnels and rooms in the ice. They can go from the house to the coal
room to the storeroom without ever being outside.

CHAPTER SEVEN

WINTER came quickly. Soon the sun was showing himself for only an hour or two every day, barely peeking above the horizon. He moved swiftly to the north, toward his wintering place behind the world. On April 23, it was only his light that we saw, shining on the mountaintops and the glaciers as though the snow was burning. Then he was gone altogether, off to his long rest.

There was only darkness after that. All day long, it was night. The air in our stable got colder and colder, and frost sometimes pushed right through the wall of hay bales. In its corner, the stove was kept lit all the time. The men skewered slabs of seal blubber onto a spike inside it, and the fat dripped slowly onto a sizzling fire, filling the stable with a stinky sort of warmth. In the stalls nearest the stove, the ponies sweated from heat, while those farthest away shivered in the chill.

I was about in the middle. I had Jehu on one side of me, and on the other quiet Snippets, who would eat just about anything he could reach, including the top rail of his stall and—once—a chunk of seal blubber.

In front of us was a corridor, then the wall of the hut. Just beyond that wall were the men, and I often heard them laugh and talk, and sometimes heard them singing. They played the piano then, with music so lively that I imagined I could see the notes flitting through the air like bright little birds. Captain Scott's voice would rise above the others, and sometimes it was his alone carrying the tune. It made me happy to hear the singing, and proud as well, because I was the one who had brought the piano.

Mr. Oates kept a schedule—he was a very clever man. As though the darkness was still divided into days, we had breakfast, lunch, and dinner, all dished out in square troughs hooked to the front of our stalls. It was a great comfort to know that a meal of chaff and oatcakes meant that it was lunchtime, because I could spend the afternoon thinking about my dinner, wondering if it would be hot mash and oil cake—my favorite—or boiled oats and chaff—my second favorite. I could never figure it out, and I was always surprised. After dinner, I thought about the hay that would come next, hoping that Patrick would be the one to bring it. Then I settled down and went to sleep thinking about breakfast, almost tasting the chaff. It made for a very busy day.

Between breakfast and lunch, if there was not a terrible blizzard, we were usually taken out for exercise. It was always nice to get out in the cold, but I liked it best when the aurora was strong and bright, filling the sky with its rivers of color, and Patrick's boots went crunch-crunch-crunch through the snow. I liked it nearly as much on the windy days, when flying snow made everything so dark that the hut disappeared if we went thirty feet away. On those nights, Patrick was enormously fat in his big bundle of clothes, and all I could see was his eyes.

But not all the ponies were winter ponies. Some of them hated to be dragged away from the blubber stove, and they tried to break loose as soon as they were out the door. Christopher was the worst for that. He was so wicked and mean that only Mr. Oates could ever try to walk him, and then it was as if Mr. Oates was trying to put a tether on a blizzard, because all we could see was a whirl of white mane and tail.

Poor Mr. Oates nearly had his arm torn off as he hauled his pony from the stable. More often than not, Christopher would be back very quickly, his rope swinging from his halter. Then Mr. Oates would arrive a long time later, always covered in snow, sometimes bruised or limping. But he never raised a hand to Christopher; he never even raised his *voice*. I believed he felt sorry for the pony, who didn't enjoy the battles any more than Mr. Oates. Christopher had never learned to trust a man, and that disappointed Mr. Oates. Patrick and the others called Christopher "a man-eater," but the pony was more terrified than most of them ever knew.

On days of blizzards, we got no exercise. For hours and hours, the wind howled around the hut. There was a tremendous rattle and bang from everything that was loose. Snow flew hard as gravel against the walls and windows of the hut, while the tarpaulins on the stable roof fluttered and banged. Inside, most of the ponies were frantic with fear. Mr. Oates never left us then. He slept in a chair pulled close to the stove, making sure we could see him and know we were safe.

I didn't like the blizzards, but there was one thing I hated even more. The silence. Through the hours when the men were sleeping, when the wind was calm, I was scared by the silence. I wished for things I'd known in the north woods: an owl's hoot, an eagle's cry, a raven's lovely gurgle. I missed the scurry of a mouse through frozen grass beneath the snow, and the dashing of a hare across a field.

Here, there was nothing like that. When the men were sleeping, the only noise in all the world was the tiny hiss from the stove, and I grew so used to that sound that I had to remind myself to listen for it. The silence sometimes drove me crazy. I started thinking about the sea ice and the Barrier, about the huge and lonely world around me. Then I thought of Weary Willy, of Blossom and Blucher lying out in the snow, so horribly alone. I thought of Guts and Nobby and Uncle Bill and saw them floating dead in the frozen sea, their eyes staring. And I thought of poor Hackenschmidt, his death such a puzzle that sometimes it didn't even seem true. I wondered if all of us would die in this place, every man and dog and pony.

All these ideas whirled through my mind like snow whipped up from the Barrier. They made me feel frightened and alone, so I pricked my ears and listened as hard as I could for the tiniest sound from the hut. If I heard the creak of the watchman's chair, I felt better. If a man snorted in his sleep or called out in a dream, I was happy. But if there was only the silence, I couldn't stand it. I rocked from side to side against the walls or knocked my hooves on the stable boards, and if that didn't bring the watchman, I started kicking at the wall.

I could make a terrific noise by kicking at the wall. The boards banged and shook; the nails came loose. Across the corridor and behind the other wall, the men woke with groans and curses, sometimes laughing too. One or the other came into the stable, and I always felt warm and safe again.

When the other ponies saw how easy it was to make the men come running, they started kicking at the wall as well. But they did it just for the sake of doing it. They hammered at the walls until the moment the stable door banged open. Then they stopped on the instant and gazed around with a look of innocence. Time and again the men came running, but in the end, they got a bit fed up and padded the walls with blankets. That muffled the sound, and took a lot of the fun away.

I liked it best when the men came to visit, especially Captain Scott. He would arrive smiling, with a pocket full of biscuits, and would stop at each stall with a pet and a treat. "Hello, Jehu. And how are you, James Pigg?" he would say. He greeted us all by name, as though we were men like him.

A good long distance from the stable, across the sea ice and along the cliff, there was a place where the men had a little wooden box that did magical things. They liked to open the box and consult with a glass stick that lived inside it. It was as thin as a worm, that little stick, with a red blood vein

143

running down its middle. But it was a clever little thing. It never spoke, yet somehow told the men just how cold it really was.

Now and then, I was taken there for exercise, between my breakfast and my lunch. There were always two men and two ponies, and the men would always try to guess the temperature as we walked along. The stick would tell them who was right.

It was a lovely walk when the sky was starry bright or flashing with aurora. The ice sparkled everywhere then. The snow crunched, and the men talked in nice low voices, and the air chilled my lungs.

At midwinter, I set out for the box with Patrick, with Victor and Birdie Bowers beside us. The sky was ablaze in sheets of blue and red. It was so beautiful that nobody spoke for a long time. We just trudged along in the crackle of icy snow.

But halfway to the box, the lights began to fade. Clouds swirled in from the Barrier, blotting out the sky. A wind began to blow against us, not strong but so cold that it froze my bones.

The men lowered their heads against it. They stopped speaking. We marched down the tracks of ponies and people.

Soon we were tramping in darkness. No stars to guide us, led only by the marks in the snow, we couldn't even see the cliffs of the Barrier. The wind whipped the snow around our feet. "Damn, it's cold," said Birdie. "Must be thirty below."

Patrick barely answered, "Nearer to forty, I'd say."

By the time we arrived at the box, a full blizzard was blowing. Birdie opened the box. He had to take off his mittens to light a match, and his hands were trembling before he could even strike a spark. Three times he tried, only to see the wind

144

snatch away his little flame. In the box, the stick watched silently.

Finally, Birdie got his fourth match burning. His hands were deep in the box, his face glowing in the tiny flame. His breaths were yellow fogs that gleamed as they drifted apart. He leaned close to the stick. "Thirty-six below," he said.

"Ah," said Patrick.

"So you were right." Birdie threw away his match. He closed the door. "And that's without the wind."

We turned our backs to the blizzard and started for the hut. The blowing snow shot past us now, though we could scarcely see it. The tracks we'd followed—even the ones we'd made ourselves just moments before—were being quickly erased. In minutes, there was nothing to guide us.

"Well, this is a fix," said Birdie Bowers.

Patrick, always the sailor, said he could steer by the wind. So he turned himself to take the blizzard on his shoulder—"by the quarter," he called it—and led us into the darkness.

The cold was taking his strength. It was slowing not only his legs but his mind. He was going in *almost* the right direction.

Of course I knew where the stable was. I didn't have to see it or smell it or hear the sounds of men and ponies. Patrick was leading us close enough that we would see the lights from the windows. We wouldn't blunder past the hut and into the terrible emptiness beyond it.

So I didn't worry at all. Until the wind changed.

It changed so slowly that Patrick didn't notice. He just turned as it shifted, step by step, and very quickly we were heading in the wrong direction altogether.

I tried to tug him to the left, but Patrick only tugged me back. I tried again. But then he pulled sharply on my tether. "Stay with me, lad," he said. "You wander off, you'll be lost."

Well, he didn't understand. We went on and on and on. I kept putting pressure on Patrick's hand, trying to swing him slowly to the left. But he was bound to keep his shoulder to the wind no matter what, and all I did was make him mad at me.

"Stop that!" he shouted the next time I pulled him.

Birdie raised his head. Great cakes of snow fell from the back of his hat. "Stop what?" he said. "What's wrong?"

"The bloody pony!" snapped Patrick. His voice was angry. "He's trying to pull me all over the country."

For a moment, his arm relaxed. I turned to the left as gently as I could. But Patrick noticed. He jerked on my halter, and the frozen leather dug painfully into my skin. "You stupid crock!" he said. "I'll leave you behind if you don't want to come."

It was terrible to have Patrick angry. I snorted and shook my head a bit to show him that I didn't mean to cause trouble. But he got mad even at that. "I'm warning you, James Pigg!" His hand came up like a club, clenched in its mitten, and he shook it in front of my eye. "What's the matter with you?" he shouted.

I had seen too many fists come at me not to shy away from his. I turned my head and skittered sideways. So Patrick wrenched me back, then marched me on faster than I wanted to go. I stumbled along, feeling sad and rotten.

Victor and Birdie fell behind us. That thickheaded pony! He was content to follow in my tracks as Patrick led the way, straight for the emptiness of the sea ice. There was one little spur of shoreline to cross, then nothing ahead but hundreds of miles of empty ice, and the sea where the killer whales lived.

I remembered a boulder that stood on the shoreline. Several times we had stopped there on the way to the box, and the men had climbed to the top of it, to sit and eat their raisins. I tried to see it in my mind, to picture exactly where it was. Then I looked at Patrick, shook my head, and made a spluttering sound with my lips.

He looked back at me, a dim shape turning in the dark. He patted my nose. "All right, lad," he said. "I'm sorry I was angry."

He stopped and stroked my ears. He brushed away the snow; he picked frosty icicles from my eyelashes. Then I nudged him with my nose as we started on again, and I turned him just a little to the right. I pressed against him in the friendly way he'd always liked, and so turned him a little bit more, so gently that he didn't notice. I steered him to the boulder, and it soon loomed in front of us—or nearly—a great mass of snow and rock.

Patrick stopped. He grabbed Birdie's arm as the little man came up beside him. "Birdie, look," he said.

Birdie recognized the boulder. "What a stroke of luck to blunder into that," he said. "A few yards in either direction and we would have walked on to our deaths."

We turned very sharply and followed the shore. Patrick was so cold and tired that he rested for a minute in a square of window light. He put one knee on the snow and hung his head, and it looked as though he was saying a prayer. Then he got up and brushed himself off, and we hurried the last little bit to the stable.

He didn't know I'd steered him. He thought blind chance had led us home, and that was fine with me.

❄   ❄   ❄

Patrick told everybody what a crock I had been on the ice. He sat the next day with Mr. Oates and Cherry, the three huddled around the stove as the blubber burned and hissed. Mr. Oates had his own place; he spent most of his time in the stable. I sometimes thought that he'd rather sit with ponies than with people.

Patrick was on his left, astride a bale of hay. "The little rogue," he called me. "A real screw he was," he said.

Of course Mr. Oates had his pipe in his teeth. The smoke drifted up in lazy curves above the stove.

"I got so angry," said Patrick. "I nearly hit him. It was horrid."

"Oh, they try everyone's patience sometimes," said Mr. Oates. "Stubborn old goats, the lot of them."

"But not Jimmy Pigg. Not usually," said Patrick. "That was what made it so strange." He held his hands toward the stove, warming his palms. "He kept pulling at me. Pulling and pulling. Why would he do that, Titus?"

Mr. Oates shrugged. He was wearing his wind helmet, as he always did in the stable. "It's hard to say what a horse thinks."

Cherry laughed. He set his glass eyes into place, twisting them on his nose. "I've determined that our ponies have the same intellect as politicians," he said.

Well, that made me very proud. A politician! I whinnied in my stall and nudged the manger board to make it rattle.

"Yes, hello there, James Pigg," said Patrick. He turned to look at me, and I was pleased to see his old smile, nearly as wide as his face.

But it was a few days later before I really knew he liked me again. It was an embarrassing moment, just at lunchtime.

The men always took away our manger boards and hung the little troughs on the next board down, so we could reach them more easily. They tied our heads with two ropes, one to each side of our stalls, to make sure we didn't steal from our neighbors.

Somehow—I wouldn't have thought it was possible—I tangled myself in my head ropes. I dribbled some mash on the floor, tried to reach it, and got all twisted around until I couldn't move.

Mr. Oates was ladling mash for Christopher. Patrick, moving ahead of him, was setting up a trough for old Snatcher. I tried to call out to them, but I couldn't make a sound. The ropes were choking me.

Mr. Oates moved down to Snatcher's trough, his ladle dripping mash. Patrick kept ahead, now lifting the manger board from Victor's stall.

I pulled at the ropes, but they only twisted more tightly. Then I lost my balance and tumbled to the floor. I hung from the ropes, and couldn't breathe at all.

For a while, I writhed and flailed. Then into my mind came an old picture: the enormous gate, the snow, the ponies' place. I hadn't thought of it since my days in the forest, but I saw it clearly, as though I was right at the gateway. It was shiny and bright, almost blinding with its sparkles. While the stable around me was fading into darkness, the gateway shone brighter than ever. It was so beautiful that I groaned.

Mr. Oates heard me. His bucket of mash clattered to the floor as he shouted, "Jimmy Pigg!" He ran down the stalls, pushing Patrick aside. He whipped a knife from his belt and cut my ropes. And as I fell to the floor, the picture of the ponies' place shimmered away into nothing.

It was Patrick who came into my stall and got me up on my feet. He rubbed my ears and stroked my neck, and he stayed with me for more than an hour. But he didn't talk until Mr. Oates left the stable. Then he threw an arm around my neck and hugged me so tightly that it nearly hurt.

"What a scare you gave me," he said. "What a fright."

He rubbed his face in my hair. "I couldn't stand it if something happened to you, lad," he said. Then he looked around, and his Irish voice dropped to a whisper. "You're a lovely lad, James Pigg."

By midwinter, the men who sat around the blubber stove hardly talked anymore. They had nothing left to say, and a friendly sort of silence hung over them. They just worked away in silence, making different types of snowshoes that they hoped would suit the ponies.

Still, once in a while a man would begin to speak, and it was always about one of two things: the South Pole or his home. He would wonder what it was like at the Pole, how long it would take to reach it, how long to get back. Or he might worry about the things in the way, like the enormous glacier called the Beardmore, with all its cliffs and crevasses. But I liked it best when the man told a little story about someone at his home. There would be a rumble of laughter for a moment then, before the silence settled in again.

As the months went by, their conversations changed a little bit. They began to connect the Pole and their homes into the same thought and tried to imagine what it would be like to finally get home from the Pole. Sometimes it pleased them, when they thought of their mothers and their wives. But sometimes it scared them, when they imagined how people would pester them to hear the story of their adventures, how their lives would suddenly be loud and busy.

I didn't like that sort of talk so much, because it always made me think of my own home. And I could never quite see how I would get back. It didn't seem possible that I would ever see the forest again, and that made me frightened and sad. I had to stomp on the floor to make the men look up, laughing, and talk of something else.

Winter stretched on and on, until it seemed that spring would never come. I wondered if the sun had died in his wintering place, and if the moon was now the king of the sky. But one day at lunchtime, a glow appeared on the distant horizon, and I knew the sun was alive and that he was waking up.

Every day, his light brightened. Then he peeked over the horizon, and a great beam of yellow light shot across the ice. The men all looked, and the men all cheered.

From then on, I thought, it would be easy. But just a day or two later, I felt a twinge in my stomach as I was standing in my stall. I looked at my belly, thinking I might see a little creature pushing at my skin from the inside. The pain shot through me, sharper than before. It made me snort and stomp my foot.

Then it got a lot worse. It felt as though the creature in there had suddenly twisted all my guts into a knot. I squealed. I tried to kick my belly to knock him away. I called out for Patrick, for Mr. Oates or Captain Scott, for anyone to come and help me.

There was no one in the stable.

The creature kept twisting and pulling my guts. I wanted to lie down, but there wasn't room. I had to fold my front legs and press my belly against the frozen earth. But that only made the thing angry, and he tried to kick me back on my feet.

My legs slipped away from under me. I bashed against the wall and flailed with my hooves.

The noise brought the watchman. He came into the stable half amused and half annoyed, thinking Nobby or Bones was up to his old tricks. He talked in a policeman's sort of voice. "Now, now, what's all this, then?"

When he saw me lying on the ground, panting and frightened, he raced from the stable, shouting for Mr. Oates.

Mr. Oates came right away and climbed straight into my stall. He hadn't even bothered with his boots but had run through the snow in his socks. There were little balls of snow stuck to the wool around his toes.

Patrick arrived behind him. He leaned over the manger board as Mr. Oates ran his hands along my belly and ribs, chasing the creature in there.

"What's wrong with him?" asked Patrick.

"I'm not certain." Mr. Oates kept pressing with his fingers. "I think it's colic."

"Is it serious?" asked Patrick.

"Sometimes. We have to get him up." Mr. Oates stood over me, straddling my neck.

Then when he pulled me up, I was so bad I tried to nip him with my teeth. I didn't mean to, but I couldn't stop myself. I wrenched my neck around to bite his wrist. I heard my teeth snap and grind. It would have meant a whipping for me with a Russian, but Mr. Oates stayed calm and gentle. "It's all right, James Pigg," he said. "You'll be right as rain in a minute."

The men got me out of the stall and into the corridor. They took me out to the ice where the aurora flickered. Mr. Oates, still in his socks, walked me in a circle. Spasm after spasm twisted through my stomach, and I didn't know if I wanted to run away or roll on my back or struggle and kick. I wanted to do them all at once. But Mr. Oates held my halter and kept me walking.

Patrick watched. "He's going to be all right," he said. "Isn't he, sir?"

"I think so. It's hard to say just yet," said Mr. Oates.

"I've promised him the Pole."

Mr. Oates looked at my friend with a strange expression. "I'll do all that I can," he said. And he did. He walked me around and around in my own tracks. He sent Patrick for a hot blanket and rubbed it on my belly. Then he said, "Patrick, do you think you might fetch my boots?"

Soon I was feeling a bit better. The creature inside still pulled at my belly, but he was fading away. I enjoyed trudging through the cold with Mr. Oates, as the southern lights danced through the sky above us. The snow crunched under our feet, and Mr. Oates talked about things that were silly and things that were not.

"So Patrick's promised you the Pole," he said. "Poor fellow. Does he really think he's going?"

A shimmer of blue spread across the sky above us. Mr. Oates watched it flicker and fade. "We can't all go trooping off toward the Pole like a lot of schoolboys. It's only a few who'll get the chance," he said. "Oh, we'll all do the work. We'll hump everything up and over that glacier. But just a few will go on from there. Just a few will get the glory."

We walked around the circle. I could feel Mr. Oates thinking, a big whirl of thoughts going through his mind.

"I'm not at all sure if I'll get the chance. But given the choice, who could say no?" he asked.

We stayed out there for hours, though the night was bitterly cold. The creature died inside me, the pain went away, and I felt like eating again. When Mr. Oates took me back to my stall, I tucked right into my dinner. Captain Scott came to see me, looking very worried. But I already felt a lot better, and by morning, I was good as new.

According to the stick in the wooden box, it was sixty degrees below zero in the winter night. Though the blubber stove sizzled away, the cold came up through the ground and filled every corner of the stable.

My skin grew itchy. Some of the other ponies were itchy

as well, and we rubbed ourselves against the walls of the stable. We rolled in the ice whenever we could. We rubbed our
hair away in great patches, but the itching went on until the
men discovered that lice were living in our hair. Then Mr.
Oates washed us down with water and tobacco, and that took
care of the lice.

Bones got colic next. He nearly died, but Mr. Oates got
him through it. And after that, there were no more troubles.
Spring was really coming, and the sun was out for hours every
day, stretching his legs across the northern sky.

Every man worked to get ready for the big push to the
Pole. Birdie Bowers sorted out his stores and supplies. Mr.
Meares began to practice with his dogs, and others tinkered
with the dreadful motor sledges.

Captain Scott supervised it all. He came nearly every day
to the stable, looked us over and talked to Mr. Oates. "I'm re-
lying on this lot," he said. "If they don't hold up, we lose the
Pole."

Mr. Oates was doing his best. He made fancy new blankets
that would keep us warmer on the Barrier. Then he tried out
different ways to stop the sun from blinding us. First he dyed
our forelocks darker. Then he made us little fringes, but Jehu
ate mine right away. So he made us bonnets instead, with vi-
sors to shield our eyes.

At the same time, Captain Scott experimented with our
snowshoes. He wanted them bigger, but not so big that they'd
trip us up. I thought they might work, but I didn't like to wear
them. It didn't feel right to walk around with baskets on my
feet. One of the sailors had a different idea, things like baggy

socks that slid right over our hooves. But he couldn't figure out how to hold them on. In the end, when Captain Scott gave up, I wasn't disappointed.

Every day, the dogs dashed around for exercise, one team racing another with their funny little sledges. The sun kept moving higher, and the days grew slowly warmer.

In the north, I had always liked to see the springtime come. All the plants put on their leaves. Animals traded their heavy coats for lighter ones. Snow disappeared, and rivers rose, and the whole world seemed to change.

But here it was different. Everything looked pretty much the same, just a little warmer and brighter.

The only thing that really changed was the men. The sun perked them up like the northern plants, making them straighter and stronger. They laughed more often, though only on the outside. I could feel their worries growing bigger and bigger as they got ready to leave for the Pole.

Amundsen has had a busy winter at the place he calls Framheim. He emerges from it with better tents and lightened sledges, with new bindings for the skis, new whips to drive the dogs along. Every man will have a face mask, every driver a chart to follow.

On August 23, with a temperature colder than forty below, he hoists the sledges from the underground workrooms where they've been readied and loaded. Each one weighs 880 pounds. He harnesses the dogs in teams of twelve and gives them their first pull of the season, three miles uphill to the starting point for the depot journeys. The old tracks of the sledges are still plain on the surface, stretching away to the south.

He unharnesses the dogs and turns them loose to run home for the hut. The rest of that day, and all the next, are spent gathering dogs that are scattered across the Barrier.

For the first time since April, the sun rises over the Barrier. With his sledges loaded at their starting point, Amundsen is ready to head off for the Pole. He is waiting only for the weather to warm.

It's the twenty-fourth of August.

      ❄   ❄   ❄

The Norwegian finds waiting less pleasant than winter. "I always have the idea that I am the only one who is left behind, while all the others are out on the road," he writes later. He records a conversation heard daily at Framheim:

"I'd give something to know how far Scott is today."

"Oh, he's not out yet, bless you! It's much too cold for his ponies."

"Ah, but how do you know they have it as cold as this? I expect it's far warmer where they are, among the mountains, and you can take your oath they're not lying idle. Those boys have shown what they can do."

CHAPTER EIGHT

MY hair at last figured out the seasons and started thinning for the summer that was now on the way. I wished it wasn't quite so quick. Already patchy from the lice, it left me rather chilly in the southern wind.

The other ponies felt the same. Winter had made us a bit lazy, and we liked to stay in the warm stable. But the men took us out two by two to get us used to working.

So the bad ponies—Nobby, Christopher, and Victor—played a mean sort of game, breaking loose whenever they could, just to see the men chase them all over the place. Like enormous rabbits, they darted from here to there. When they got tired of that and went back to the stable, the other bad ponies cheered them with squeals and kicks.

The worst was Christopher—of course. He made life a misery for poor Mr. Oates, who was always so patient and kind. Christopher tried to wreck the sledges; he tried to bite the men. He sometimes had four of them struggling all at once to wrestle him into his harness. I thought he was wicked and savage, but it was still sad to see him when he'd lost the battle. Down on his knees with his front legs hobbled, his great chest shaking as he breathed, he looked broken. But he kept a look of defiance in his eyes, and he started up again the first chance he got.

❋   ❋   ❋

The sun came back at the end of August. In September, we began our training runs.

The stronger ponies, like Uncle Bill and Snatcher and Bones, went happily back to work, heaving their sledges through the new snow. For me, it was a bit of a struggle. I found the surface too soft, the air too cold. For Jehu, it was nearly impossible.

He looked tired. He looked old and miserable. Captain Scott was very worried about the little pony and decided that Jehu was too weak for the trek to the Pole. Scott had him unharnessed and put back in the stable.

Jehu was pleased at first, until he realized that he was going to be left behind when the rest of us struck out for the Pole. At the thought of that, he found a new strength, and from then on pulled just as hard as old Chinaman. Why, he pulled nearly as hard as me!

In October, everything was ready. We waited only for the weather, for the snow to harden on the ice.

Captain Scott sent off the motor party first, in the middle of the month. The two machines, with four men to help them, went banging across the ice, farting puffs of smoke.

The men cheered. Even I, who hated the motors, felt something stir inside me as I watched them crawl away toward the Pole, flinging up snow from their rotating runners. They seemed like brave and steadfast things dragging their little sledges, willing to march forever.

Big Taff Evans was amazed. "My, sir," he said to Captain Scott. "I reckon if them things can go on like that, you wouldn't want nothing else."

But even as we watched and waved, the first machine broke down. It sat quiet and sullen, bleeding oil onto the snow. The men carried a bit of it back for repairs, as though they'd saved the heart of the thing.

I didn't sleep that night, knowing that I'd be on my way in the morning. Our sledges were waiting, our traces were sorted out. Birdie Bowers was going over his stores one more time, and Captain Scott was checking lists.

In my stall I heard the wind rise. I heard it whine and moan. Soon came the patter of whirling snow, and I knew a blizzard had begun.

It buried the sledges. It covered the trail to the lonely place and pinned us down for days.

On the twenty-third of October, the motor sledges tried again, only to break down for a second time at the edge of the ice. Captain Scott was terribly disappointed. But after a night's rest, the motors must have felt a bit better, because they went roaring away on the twenty-fourth, over the ice and around the tongue of the glacier.

There was another wait for us, as another blizzard blew, and it wasn't until the last day of the month that our journey began.

The teams of dogs went first, one driven by Mr. Meares, the other by his Russian. Untroubled by the hollows and drifts of fresh snow, the dogs took off at a run, barking like lunatics.

Captain Scott watched them rather sadly. He shuffled his feet in the snow, his head hanging down, and he looked to me like a boy who had lost a great game.

An hour later, I was the very first pony to strike out for the Pole. I thought it was a great honor, and I didn't understand why I shared it only with Jehu, and not with any other ponies. Little Jehu was the weakest of all, so worn down by the winter that Captain Scott feared he might not even make it to the lonely place. This was a test, not a journey, for Jehu. If he couldn't travel this first little bit, he would be left behind.

I liked Jehu. He was quiet and gentle. He always did what he was told. But best of all, he was slower than me. With Jehu, I never had to worry about falling behind.

"Ready, James Pigg?" asked Patrick that day. We stood outside the hut—two ponies and two men. He held on to my rope, and together we took our first step to the Pole. Behind us, Jehu followed with Mr. Atkinson. It was very exciting. Never before in my life had I been a leader.

We took our second step. We took our third. I thought I might count them all the way to the Pole, just to see how many there were. But after seven, I forgot.

162

Our sledges were lightly loaded. We followed the tracks of the motor sledges, through fresh snow that lay in rolling drifts. Underneath, the ice was good and solid, and we had none of the trouble we'd seen before. There were no holes to swallow me up, no killer whales to drag me down. In less than six hours, we reached the old hut at the lonely place, and though Jehu was breathing heavily—well, so was I—he surprised the men by moving along so quickly.

❋   ❋   ❋

The old hut at the lonely place had a wide verandah. The men took us straight up the steps and left us tethered to a post under its roof. They soon had a fire burning inside, with smoke drifting from the stovepipe.

It was a very cold night. I expected to shiver right through it, unsleeping. The wind gusted around the corners of the hut and whirled under the roof above me. When Patrick came out through the door, I hoped he was bringing more blankets, maybe one that he'd heated by the stove if I was very lucky. But his hands were empty.

He untied my tether line. "Come along, James Pigg," he said, tugging me forward.

I didn't want to go down to the snow, into the wind. There wasn't a lot of shelter where I was, but I did have a little, and I wished I could stay there. But if Patrick wanted me out on the snow-covered ice, that was where I'd go. I followed him along the verandah, my hooves clomping on the wood.

"Good lad," he said.

To my huge surprise, we didn't go down to the snow. At

the door, we turned the other way and went right inside the hut. It was warm in there, nicely lit with paraffin lamps. It smelled of spice and beef, because Mr. Atkinson was making dinner on a Primus stove that roared away on a table. Patrick left me in the middle of the room and went back to fetch little Jehu.

I had always wondered what it was like in a house. I had imagined a stable for people, with stalls for sleeping, troughs for eating, because that was all I'd ever known. I didn't know that men had padded beds stacked one above another, or lots of chairs, and little things scattered all around. I watched Patrick eat his dinner. Then I watched him stretch out on a bed and read a book.

It was so warm and pleasant in there that I hoped the snow would bury the hut, that the four of us could live inside it forever. I thought what a very different life I'd come to, and what a fortunate little pony I was.

Mr. Atkinson lay down on a different bed. He stuffed a pipe with tobacco and lit it, then puffed big bubbles of smoke toward the ceiling. I watched Patrick turn the pages of his book. He turned quite a few before he looked at me over the top of them. I could see in his eyes that he was smiling. "Hello, James Pigg," he said.

Mr. Atkinson blew another smoke bubble. It rolled up from his mouth and flattened on the ceiling. "That pony never takes his eyes off you," he said. "Have you noticed that, Patrick? He adores you."

"Well, now, I don't see why," said Patrick, all red and smiling. He lowered his book and looked right back.

I could feel his fondness for me. At that moment, I was almost overcome with happiness. But his next words crushed me.

"You know, he doesn't seem as bad as Titus says. Or Scott. Not to me, he doesn't." Patrick turned his head to look at Mr. Atkinson. "He's not such a crock, is he?"

Mr. Atkinson sighed. "I'm no judge of horses," he said. "He's better than mine, no doubt. But that's not saying a lot."

With that, Mr. Atkinson put away his pipe. He wriggled down into his sleeping bag, drawing the top of it right over his head. Jehu stood beside me, muzzling his own feet to pick away the loose skin.

"He's such a plucky little fellow," said Patrick, watching me again. "I think he's strong enough to reach the Pole. I think he'll do it. And don't I know him better than anyone else?"

Mr. Atkinson grunted. "I'm not sure that it matters," he said in a sleepy voice.

"What do you mean?" asked Patrick.

"I don't believe *any* of them will get to the Pole."

That surprised me. It surprised Patrick too. "Why not?" he asked.

"Up the Beardmore? I just can't see ponies trekking up a glacier." Mr. Atkinson yawned again and rolled over in the sleeping bag. He looked like a big caterpillar. "I don't think Scott will try it."

Mr. Atkinson was a doctor. His interests were tapeworms and things, not ponies. I thought he was talking rubbish, but Patrick believed him. "Do you mean they'll turn back?" he asked. "At the Beardmore? Will *I* have to turn back too?"

There was no answer from Mr. Atkinson, only a muffled sort of grunt that might have been a snore. Outside, a gust of wind whistled around the roof. Beside me, Jehu raised his head and made a muttering sound with his lips.

"They *will* turn back, won't they?" asked Patrick.

He sounded worried now, but I didn't know why. If we couldn't go up the glacier, we would *have* to turn back. What choice could there be?

The others arrived in the afternoon of the next day, just before another blizzard. I saw them through the window, a long line of men and ponies and sledges weaving out from a thickening sky. All the sledges were lightly loaded, and the big ponies moved quickly. Snatcher was in the lead, plowing steadily through the drifts. Way at the back was Chinaman, plodding along like an old woman.

That night, as the wind blasted, three ponies stayed in the hut. Chinaman kept waking the men by stamping on the floor, but no one turned him out into the blizzard. They just lay with their hands over their ears, sometimes laughing and sometimes cursing.

It was a pleasant night despite the wind, away from the wretched dogs, who had stayed behind at the winter station with Mr. Meares and the Russian. I would have liked to stay longer at the lonely place, now that it wasn't so lonely. But with the Barrier covered in fresh snow, we moved out late in that same day, to travel in the coldest hours.

When I was sent first, with Jehu and Chinaman, I knew for

certain that I was a crock. We were so slow that we needed a head start. Mr. Oates and the others were just beginning to wrestle with Christopher when Patrick led me off. He carried a compass but watched for the fading tracks of the motor sledges, now just shallow bands that were sometimes hard to see.

The sun swooped low and disappeared as we walked along to the south. But soon he rose again and wheeled across the sky as though in a great hurry to get ahead of us. Patrick had his goggles on, while I wore my new dark fringes clipped to my halter. The gleam of the Barrier shimmered right through them, but it was hard to see very much. When Patrick called out to the others—"What's that up there, do you think?"—I had to squint and turn my head, and I still couldn't tell what he was looking at.

Mr. Atkinson came up beside us. He lifted his goggles and held a hand above his eyes as Jehu nibbled at my shoulder. "Hard to tell in this light," he said. "I think it's a tent. Seems a long way away."

We hurried a bit, over snow that the wind had smoothed as flat as a floor. But the thing wasn't far away at all. And it wasn't even a tent. The sun's strange light made everything look tall that day, and more distant than it was. After just a hundred yards, we reached an empty fuel tin with a bit of rolled-up paper stuck in its spout.

There was a message from the motor party written on the paper: *Hope to meet at 80° 30'*. Mr. Atkinson looked at the date on the note. "They're five days ahead," he said. "They're doing jolly well, aren't they?"

He sounded jealous. He sighed as he stared down at

the ghostly tracks of the two machines. They must have been far ahead, rattling on and on across the snowy waves, never slowing down, never getting tired, towing their sledges in dead-straight lines. It seemed funny to think of sledges dragging sledges. But I envied them myself. I had to tug and tug to get my own sledge moving again. The crossbar thumped against my legs. Patrick helped with a little pull on the traces, and away we went with Jehu and Chinaman puffing behind us.

The wind fell as we marched, and by the time we stopped, it was calm. The sun glared his light off the snow, trying to trick us into thinking the air was warmer than it really was. He could fool my back, but not my feet and my belly. They knew very well how cold it was.

I felt a bit tired after the first day on the Barrier. But Chinaman and Jehu were much worse. They didn't eat, and couldn't sleep, but just stood and shivered in the sun, their backs glistening with sweat that was partly frozen, partly thawed.

The other ponies arrived soon after us. The big ones like Snatcher and Bones and Christopher came charging into camp, snorting like killer whales, their handlers half running beside them. Their heavy sledges—three-quarter tons full— rocked and jolted along. Little Michael, Nobby, and the rest drew up in a straggling bunch, with Captain Scott at the very back, leading a sad-looking Snippets.

There were ten of us gathered together. Ten ponies tied in a row along the picket line. It was strange to think that I'd been in the very same place before the winter, just starting out, in a group of eight. And of those eight, only me and

Nobby were left. I wondered if the same thing might happen again.

Many of the ponies looked older now; some were gray and patchy. The men seemed older too, not laughing anymore as they'd laughed the last time we were here. No one talked about the books they were reading. No one talked very much at all.

❄ ❄ ❄

The next day, not far from camp, we found a dark spot on the snow. Patrick took off a mitten and touched it with his fingertip.

"Oil," he said. "Must be bleeding from one of those motor sledges."

Soon there was a trail of the motor's blood, drop after drop, that led us right to the sledge itself. It lay dead on the snow, quiet and cold and still. The poor old thing, I thought. It had staggered on for a long way. It had gone as far as it could go, then fallen in its tracks, just like Weary Willy.

There were ruts in the snow, and footprints all around. It was easy to see what had happened. The drivers had harnessed themselves to the motor's sledge and gone on with the other machine, pulling like horses. There were deep gouges in the snow where they'd struggled to get the thing moving. It must have been nearly as heavy as mine.

We left the motor lying on top of the snow, its parts strewn around as though wolves had got at it. And we went on again, into a rising wind.

I expected another blizzard. The men made another

169

monstrous wall at the camp and I huddled behind it, shivering. But instead of snow came a white haze, and the coldest weather I'd seen for a while. I shook until my bones were rattling.

I thought of the motor sledge lying abandoned on the Barrier. Then at last I fell asleep, and I dreamed a bad dream. I was back in the forest, in the grassy place with all my old herd around me, my mother at my side. It was the day the men had come to catch me, and I knew it was going to happen; I knew the men were coming. But I couldn't stop it. Then I saw the silvery stallion towering up.

It was just like the way it had happened, except the men were on foot, and they were Mr. Oates and Captain Scott and Patrick. The stallion shrieked and kicked. Then Patrick saw me across the clearing and came walking toward me. I was more scared in my dream than I'd been in the meadow. I didn't want to be captured. But in my dream I couldn't run; I couldn't even move. Patrick tried to tempt me with a biscuit that he held out in his hand. "Come on now," he said, stepping slowly closer. "There's a good lad."

I woke up as he touched me. I woke up and there he was. He stood right in front of me with a bit of biscuit in his fingers. He was smiling, happy to see me. But I thought I was in the forest, not out on the Barrier behind the big pony wall, and I believed he'd come to capture me. I pulled away, confused and afraid, meaning to dash for the trees, just as I'd done when I was very young. But I only tugged against the tether line, with a shock that made me scream. I startled Jehu beside me, who startled Christopher, who wheeled away with his hooves flashing.

I reared up. And without meaning to, I struck out at

Patrick. My knees slammed against his chest. The biscuit flew from his hand as he fell backward.

He landed flat on the snow, and suddenly there was a look of dread in his eyes, of fear that I was about to stomp him right into the snow. He even held up a hand to save himself.

I lowered my head, of course. I blinked my eyes; I licked my lips, my tongue flickering like a snake's. I wanted Patrick to know I would never hurt him, not for the whole world. He could get up and beat me if he wanted, and all I would do was stand there and wait for him to finish.

But he crawled away from me. On his back. Using his elbows for levers, pushing with his feet. And that look of fear stayed in his eyes until he had gone far enough that I couldn't possibly reach him. Then he stood up—slowly—and he said in a whisper, "What's the matter with you, Jimmy Pigg? What's wrong with you, lad?"

I ached to feel his hand on my nose, but I knew he didn't trust me. I could see that in the way he stood, in the way he held his hands. I snorted and moved closer, and he only moved away. He went back to the tents, where the men were up and working, getting ready for the march. When he came later to put on my harness, his hands trembled all the time he stood beside me.

I was as gentle as a rabbit. I made no sound; I didn't move a muscle. But still Patrick smelled of nervousness. He kept talking, yet his voice was different. "Easy now," he said. "Easy now." He said it again and again, like a bird with its call. "Easy now."

I was afraid that he would never trust me again. I was afraid he didn't like me anymore. When we set out with Jehu and Chinaman, it was the same as all the other days, and terribly different too. Patrick didn't stand so close to me. He led me by my rope instead of my halter. If I stumbled or lurched, he was quick to leap even farther away.

We went along for hours. They all seemed long and sad, as though time had turned to a sort of mush that I had to slosh aside. I kept remembering the way Patrick had looked up at me from the ground, and I felt like a rotten old apple, all brown and horrid inside. I wished Patrick could know that he'd scared me out of a dream. And then, quite suddenly, he let go of the rope and took my halter instead. His glove slipped under the leather strap, back into its old place. His head tipped sideways and pressed against me. I pushed back. I snorted softly.

"Oh, James Pigg," he said. "Did I startle you this morning? Is that what it was?" He tightened his hand. He whispered to me. "You're a good lad, James Pigg."

I wanted to believe that Patrick knew what I was thinking. But it seemed a little bit impossible. No man had ever done that—or even bothered to try. But no man had ever cared for me like Patrick did.

❄   ❄   ❄

At the end of the march that day, we came to Corner Camp. The men dug out the buried supplies and loaded our sledges. They uncovered bales of forage that had been under the snow for nine months and let us chew away. I thought it was delicious. The frozen stems crackled in my teeth.

Each pony tucked into the fodder as he arrived at the

camp. We went at it like pigs, even turning down our oil cakes to feast on the fodder.

As I stood eating by the wall, I watched Christopher come into the camp with Mr. Oates. The man kept a firm hand on his rope, not giving the pony an inch to spare. The crossbar swayed and hit the snow. The pony stepped higher, faster, as though trying to outrun it. So Mr. Oates checked him with a sharp pull on the rope. Then Christopher kicked out with his hind legs and tried to skitter sideways.

In a flash, I was thinking of the crowds at the horse fair. I heard the noise and the shouts and the cries of the horses. I remembered a man trying to pull a boy by the hand, the boy not wanting to go. He had leaned back, digging his heels into the ground, screaming as he struggled and squirmed.

Christopher was just like that boy. All the way across the snow, he tried to buck and kick, to run away. Mr. Oates stared grimly ahead, marching along—for once like a soldier.

It took four men to get Christopher out of his harness. The mean pony fought them all, like a bear in a pack of wolves. I hated to see it. I hated to hear it. Christopher whirled himself around, trying to bite at every arm and leg that came near him, and he didn't give up until he was exhausted, until he stood bent and heaving, as trembly as a shrew.

I understood it then. Christopher was terrified.

The men thought he was mean. They thought he was vicious and angry. But the pony was only frightened, scared of his harness, of the feel of the sledge dragging behind him, of the trapped sort of feeling that came with the collar and traces. He was so scared of men that he couldn't stand to have one beside him holding his halter or rope. Of course he struggled!

Of course he fought! I wished Captain Scott would see it for himself. And poor Mr. Oates. I saw him staring at the pony with tears in his eyes, because he hated the battles just as much as Christopher did.

At Corner Camp, Mr. Oates had a good look at all the ponies. I was feeling a bit stronger, and I was glad that he noticed. "Much improved," he said, smiling proudly. He told Captain Scott that I was getting fitter from my exercise. But he said the same for Jehu and Chinaman, and I thought they looked a little worse every day.

When I left that camp, I was pulling nearly five hundred pounds. I remembered the last time I was here, when Captain Scott had pointed the way to the Pole, a straight line across the Barrier. Even he looked different now, a little bit thinner and a lot more worried. As he trudged along ahead of me, leading the way to the south, I thought his wish to reach the Pole was stronger than ever. He would do it, I thought, no matter what it meant for his dogs and ponies, and maybe even for his men.

❄ ❄ ❄

We found the body of the last motor sledge just a little way from the camp. The drivers had left another note saying they were going ahead, man-hauling for One Ton Depot.

We passed the thing in a strange sort of mist that shone with a white light. The men in goggles, the ponies with their fringes on, we marched steadily south.

The wind rose slowly. But soon we were leaning against it, our heads down again as blowing snow whipped up around us.

We camped early, too cold to go on. The wind became a

blizzard, piling snow against the pony wall, thrashing the sides of the tents till the canvas shook and boomed.

Captain Scott came out of his tent and stood all alone in the wind. With his hands behind his back, he squinted terribly into the blizzard. Then he came and stood among the ponies, as though trying to see for himself how much shelter we got from the wall. He put his hand on my back, at the edge of the blanket, in the snow-clotted tangles of my mane.

A feeling of gloom came out of him. I could feel it through his hand, a sense of gathering despair, or of dwindling hope. Then he looked toward the wind with an angry face, as though the wind was a person, as though the blizzard was blowing just to annoy him.

The snow gusted around us, over the wall. It piled up on my blanket. It piled up on the ground and banked against the tents, against the sledges and the fodder bales. When Captain Scott took his hand from my back, his mitten was white with snow.

I twitched my ears. Beside me, Jehu was doing the same thing. He swung his head to the north, toward the faintest sounds.

Out of the blizzard came the dogs. Faint and gray in the whirling snow, their faces caked with white, they ran at an easy lope. The sledges slid along, and I saw the men running beside them, made fat in their sledging clothes. I heard the Russian commands called out against the wind, and the words sent my old fears shivering through me.

The men veered to the right and stopped. They made their camp downwind of ours, and the dogs started up a mournful howling that sounded far too much like wolves.

Captain Scott was watching them, his hand moving like a brush to keep the snow from his eyes.

"So they *can* travel in this," he said to himself. "Still, you can't trust them. It's ponies you want on the Barrier." He turned to face me. He took off his mitten and thrust his bare hand under my blanket, trying to feel how much snow had gathered there. He kept talking in sad tones. "The motors are gone. The dogs can't last. It's up to you lot now."

He pulled out his hand. He tightened the edges of my blanket, then gave me a solid and friendly thump. "My life's in your hands, James Pigg," he said.

At Framheim, the change in weather comes incredibly quickly. In the first week of September, the temperature plummets from −43.6 to −63.4, then soars to −20.2 The next day it's −7.6.

"At last the change had come, and we thought it was high time," writes Amundsen. "Every man ready, tomorrow we are off."

It doesn't go quite as smoothly as he plans. The dogs are rambunctious. Two of the teams bolt and have to be rounded up. It's more than an hour past noon when they leave, and Amundsen almost turns back right away because three puppies are following the sledges. But he decides to go on, believing the puppies will turn around.

The old tracks of the sledges fade away on the windswept Barrier, but the drivers pick up the line of flags that were planted in the fall and follow them easily. "The going was splendid," Amundsen says of that day, "and we went at a rattling pace to the south."

He tells that the teams did not go far: "eleven and three-quarter miles." But that's only two hours' running. The Norwegians pitch their camp at three-thirty in the afternoon.

"The first night out is never very pleasant, but this time it was awful," writes Amundsen. "There was such a row going on among our ninety dogs that we could not close our eyes. It was a blessed relief when four in the morning came round, and we could begin to get up. We had to shoot the three puppies when we stopped for lunch that day."

Chapter Nine

IN bright sunshine, with a cold wind blowing, we followed the old cairns across the Barrier. It was a good day's march with ten miles covered. But the crocks and I were going a bit slowly, and the others caught us up in the afternoon, with a mile or two to go.

Christopher came first. He thundered past with his breaths puffing white, his great hooves slamming the snow. Mr. Oates held his tether, but the pony led the man, barreling on as if he was heading for his stable. Victor was close behind him, with little Birdie Bowers trotting at his side. Snatcher followed, then Nobby and Michael. They all went by, one by one, last of all Captain Scott and Snippets.

I felt sorry for Patrick, stuck at the back with me and the

crocks, and I pressed myself harder, digging in with my hooves. But he held me back.

"It's all right, James Pigg," he said. "You're doing just fine."

A moment later, Mr. Wright called out from behind us: "Hold up a minute, will you? I think my sledge meter's jammed."

We stopped and waited. Patrick fed me a little piece of biscuit that he found in his pocket. Then I heard Chinaman whinny, and turned my head to see him standing by himself in his harness. Mr. Wright was clearing snow from the wheel that trailed behind his sledge. The pony whinnied again—a sad sound. He didn't like to be left alone back there, with the big ponies far ahead. Christopher, in the lead, had crossed a wave of snow and was slipping away behind it.

Chinaman snorted. I heard a jingle from his buckles, a rattle from the sledge, a sudden shout from Mr. Wright. Then Chinaman went galloping past us. It startled me to see him rushing past, going as fast as he could go across the Barrier.

"Wait! Wait!" shouted Mr. Wright. And a moment later, *he* went past us, running flat out, with his mittens flying from their tethers. His long legs sprang like a cricket's as he bounded across the snow. "Stop!" he shouted.

But Chinaman kept running. And Mr. Wright kept chasing him. And suddenly, Jehu, with a toss of his head, broke loose from Mr. Atkinson and went running after the both of them.

Mr. Atkinson was too surprised to move. He gaped at the three figures loping over the snow, and then he started laughing. Patrick laughed as well, and up ahead, the men looked back and saw the two old ponies plowing along in their wild sort of canter, with Mr. Wright racing between them, and soon the sound of laughter filled the wide Barrier.

Nobody had thought Chinaman remembered how to run, he was so old. They had given up on Jehu right at the start, and now rewarded the little pony with a nickname: the Barrier Wonder.

That was the nicest day of all, everyone happy as they pitched their tents and built the pony walls. I hoped every day would be like that, but the next morning took us back into misery.

Strong winds made the marching very cold. Then a blizzard stopped us after only five miles and covered the Barrier with fresh snow that made the slogging harder when we started out again.

All of us bogged in the pits of snow, but again the bigger ponies passed me. Chinaman had to struggle for every yard, heaving huge breaths, with his ribs bending in and out. He didn't have the strength to keep the sledge moving, so hurled himself at the harness to shift it along a foot at a time.

Mr. Wright tried to help him, but there wasn't much he could do. When we staggered into camp, he asked Mr. Oates to have a look at Chinaman. "It's not proper to drive him like this," he said.

Mr. Oates examined the pony. "That's the fellow. That's the soldier," he said as he moved from tail to head.

Mr. Wright hovered nearby. "It doesn't look good for him, does it?" he asked.

"Frankly, it doesn't look good for any of them," said Mr. Oates. He rubbed Chinaman's shoulder. "You should be proud of this one. He's done very well."

"But how much farther can he go?" asked Mr. Wright. "Another mile or two, and that's it?"

"Oh, I think he's got days yet," said Mr. Oates. "His spirits are good, and that's the thing. It isn't muscle and bone that will carry him on, you know. It's spirit."

"But to make him work till the end . . ." Mr. Wright let his voice fall away. "To the very end?"

"He would want nothing less," said Mr. Oates. He walked along the tether line, stopping again at Jehu. I snorted, trying to call him closer. "Yes, I see you there, James Pigg," he said.

Mr. Atkinson followed him. "It seems so calculated," he said.

"Well, you see, you're thinking like a person, Silas. You want to think like a horse instead." Mr. Oates touched a finger to his head, tapping through the wool of his balaclava. "There's a lot of bone up there, but not much else. Believe me."

Well, that seemed a bit insulting. But I didn't mind too much if it came from Mr. Oates.

He ran his hand down Jehu's neck, up across the pony's ribs, down again along the flank. All the time, he kept walking toward me.

"Most men—most people—want the same thing," he told Mr. Wright. "A good life of good work, then out to pasture—in our own way—until the end arrives some long time later. But not so for a horse, and a pony's surely no different."

He was smiling at me now as he reached up his hands to my forehead. "The saddest horses I've ever seen are the ones put out to pasture," he said. "They get listless, they get fat, they stand by the fence forever, looking out at the world they knew. They're trapped by that fence, you see. People think the pasture's a kindness. But to a horse it's a prison."

Mr. Wright sighed. "Do you believe that truly?"

"I do," said Mr. Oates. "A horse doesn't dream of the pastures. If anything it lives in dread of them."

He was almost right. I did not dream of pastures, when pastures were fields of dirt and nibbled-down grass and rusty old buckets to drink from. But I didn't dream of harnesses, either. I worked because it pleased him, and because it pleased Patrick and Captain Scott and all the others who had been very kind.

Mr. Oates rubbed his hand down the long flat of my nose, then cupped it under my mouth. I snorted. I made the happiest sounds that I knew, but to the men, it was just a murmuring flutter of lips and gums.

Mr. Wright chuckled. "You'd think he's trying to talk to you."

"In his way, he is," said Mr. Oates.

I lowered my head to let him rub the space between my ears.

"I understand horses better than I understand people," he said. "I prefer their company most of the time, to be honest. And if there's one thing I've learned, it's this: A horse would sooner die in harness than rot in a field."

Mr. Wright didn't look convinced. He came up beside Mr. Oates and idly stroked my nose. "Aren't you giving them your own thoughts?"

"Only because we think the same way," said Mr. Oates. "Soldiers and horses. We don't hope to die old."

He was so nearly right. I didn't want to die old if it meant being alone and frightened. But it wasn't the harness that made me work, or the tether that stopped me from running away. Christopher was proof of that, with all his fears and battles. If I had the choice, I would rather grow old with

Mr. Oates. But I'd sooner die in harness than disappoint him. Not that it seemed to matter much. Everything was already decided, and a pony didn't have many choices to make.

❄   ❄   ❄

The next day's march brought us to the place where Blucher was buried. The flagstaff still marked the spot, and all around it the snow was fresh and deep. It was an eerie place, with the little pole tipping in the wind, back and forth, as though Blucher was pushing up from below, trying to struggle from his icy grave.

Chinaman had never been there. I watched as he veered from his path ahead of me, pulling Mr. Atkinson sideways till he stood right above the grave. He made a sad sort of whine, then pawed the snow gently with a forefoot. His gesture made me think of my mother, when she had helped me to my feet on my first day on Earth.

Mr. Atkinson frowned. He didn't know that Blucher was buried there. But Patrick did, and he looked at Chinaman with astonishment. When the pony whined again, he seemed almost afraid. "This gives me the willies," he said. "Let's get him away from here."

It took a few tugs to get the old pony moving. Chinaman didn't want to leave that place. Then he kept looking back, turning his head this way and that way, still making the sad little cries that had spooked Patrick.

A hundred yards on, he stopped altogether. He stomped his feet in the snow, raised his head, and let out a shrill sort of shriek. It was the cry I'd known, when I was young, as the gathering call of the silvery stallion.

I was sure that Chinaman was calling to Blucher. And I was sure that Patrick knew it. My friend's breaths came a little more quickly. His hand tightened on my halter, as though he didn't want me to look back, or was afraid to look back himself, in case he saw the ghost of Blucher rising gray and shimmering from the snow.

❄ ❄ ❄

Storm followed storm. It snowed, it stopped, it snowed again as we made our way south from one old camp to another. The Barrier was either hidden by blizzards or veiled in the white mist that blinded men and ponies. We saw no land for days, but trekked along, guided by the compass, from one old cairn to the next.

Mr. Wright kept thinking that every mile was the last for his old pony. But Mr. Oates was right, of course. Both Chinaman and Jehu kept slogging on, though the going got worse all the time. I could see that neither pony would last much longer, but they kept pushing themselves on, not wanting to be left behind. Patrick kept telling me, "You're doing well, James Pigg. You're a good lad." But I was getting tired too. I felt nearly as old as Chinaman.

We reached Bluff Depot, where I had turned back the year before with poor old Blucher and Blossom. We picked up the supplies they had dragged so far, and we carried them on to the south. A day later, Patrick gave me half an oil cake in the middle of the march and told me, "You've come a hundred miles, James Pigg."

Then we went another fifty.

Even the strongest ponies were starting to wear out, but we struggled every day in a line that stretched far along the Barrier. Then we reached One Ton Depot, where Captain Scott had buried his last supplies the summer before, where he'd turned back to spare his ponies.

I could see the old wall where Guts and Punch and Uncle Bill had sheltered. The marks of their hooves were still punched through the snow around the big cairn that marked the place. All of them were dead, but that wall still stood.

Nobby had been there. But if he was sad, he didn't show it. He barely glanced at the wall, then watched the men get out their shovels and stared at one little spot on the snow. He never took his eyes from it, and as soon as the men went near it, he whinnied with excitement.

Patrick was putting my blanket on my back just then. He heard Nobby's shrill cry, saw him watching the digging, and I felt his hands tremble at the edge of my blanket. "Now, what's buried there?" he asked himself.

The men dug through the snow, then dropped their shovels and knelt by the hole they'd made. When they reached into the snow, Nobby shrieked again, stomping his little hooves. Then Patrick laughed as the men brought up a bale of frozen fodder.

There was a lot of pony food buried there at One Ton Depot. We had a day of rest as the men sorted out the supplies and rearranged the sledges. Captain Scott had long talks with the men, making plans for "the march on the summit," as he called it. He lightened the loads for Jehu and Chinaman, and added to Christopher's, to Michael's, to the other strong ponies. He lightened mine as well, making me think that I might be part of the dash. But when we trekked away to the south, I saw that the men had saved weight by leaving out forage and oil cakes, and that made no sense to me. How were we supposed to eat, I wondered, if the food was far behind us?

When we trekked away toward the south, a huge amount of pony food still sat on the snow. I thought of pulling on my tether to make Patrick see it. But he could hardly have missed the bales of fodder, the boxes of biscuits, lying as though abandoned.

The sun made it harder for us. He filled the sky with a terrible glare, a brightness that softened the surface until even Christopher was exhausted by plunging through hollows where the snow was soft as swamp mud.

Icicles grew from our nostrils again. Mr. Wright used his windproof jacket to cover Chinaman's nose, to shield his pony from the cold wind.

Thirteen miles a day. That was the goal set by Captain Scott, and we struggled along to meet it. But me and Jehu and Chinaman barely managed to keep ahead of the others. As the men packed up our lunchtime camps, we could see Christopher plodding up along our tracks with Mr. Oates beside him. When we stopped at the end of the march, we could hear the dogs coming quickly from the distance.

Every handler fussed over his pony to keep us warm behind our walls, blanketed and fed. But just as Mr. Oates had said, it was only spirit that kept Chinaman moving. Every day, I could see dread in his eyes as Mr. Wright backed him into his harness. Then off he went with a grim determination. The men began to call him Thunderbolt, a name they used with both amusement and admiration.

I led the way. My hooves left tracks where there were no tracks. In the hours around midnight, when the sun was low and the day was coldest, I punched through the soft crust that froze on the Barrier. With the steady pace that Patrick set, the sound was like the drumming of a faraway army. I was proud to be the leader, breaking trail for every pony from worn-out old Jehu to the fierce Christopher. Even Captain Scott walked in the tracks I made.

I was the one who found the cairn as big as a mountain, towering so high from the snow that I saw it from more than nine miles away. I found the motor party camped just beyond it, the men in their seventh day of waiting. They had dragged their sledge nearly as far as I had dragged mine. And now they fell in with us and dragged it some more, heaving together in the harness. They were hungry and tired, nearly as thin as Jehu.

I was pleased that I could help Jehu. He plodded in my tracks, down the grooves of my sledge runners. He could hardly haul the sledge, although his load had been lightened again and again, and now a team of dogs could have hauled it easily. He could barely lift his hooves.

He looked worse than the tired old mare who had wandered away from my band of ponies. But he never slowed, or never stopped to rest. He just walked along, one step at a time, as though his legs were parts of an engine.

Four days out from Framheim, Amundsen's dogs reach their full vigor. They run nearly out of control, eager to go forward. The drivers have to slow them down. Teams collide and the dogs get into terrible fights.

Then the temperature drops, and it's suddenly sixty-eight below. "One's breath was like a cloud," says Amundsen later. "And so thick was the vapor over the dogs that one could not see one team from the next, though the sledges were being driven close to one another."

The men can take the cold. Amundsen says that at times it even feels too warm. But he worries about the dogs.

"In the morning, especially, they were a pitiful sight," he says. "They lay rolled up as tightly as possible, with their noses under their tails, and from time to time one could see a shiver run through their bodies; indeed, some of them were constantly shivering. We had to lift them up and put them into their harness. I had to admit

that with this temperature it would not pay to go on; the risk was too great."

Amundsen decides to turn back at his depot at 80 degrees south. He reaches it on the fourteenth of September, empties his sledges, and races back to the sea.

Along the way, he turns loose the dogs that can't keep up, trusting them to find their own way home.

CHAPTER TEN

JEHU was dying, and everyone knew it. He had worked till the end of his days.

But Mr. Atkinson was terribly sad, and he believed it was a cruelty to push the pony any farther. So on the morning of the twenty-fourth of November, at the end of a night's long march, Mr. Atkinson fed his little pony a biscuit. He combed the forelock with his fingers, then petted Jehu one last time.

Mr. Oates had the pistol. He led the pony away from the rest of us, making quiet little clucking sounds as he did it. A few of the men, like Cherry, gave Jehu a pet as he passed. "Good lad," they said. "Well done," they told him.

Jehu looked back, puzzled because Mr. Atkinson wasn't going along with him. But Mr. Atkinson didn't see that. He had turned his back on the pony and was rubbing his ears as

191

if they were cold. I thought he was masking the sound of Jehu's wheezing breaths.

Suddenly, all of the men were busy with little jobs. Captain Scott had to nip into his tent for a moment. Birdie Bowers had to crouch down beside his sledge and tug at the lashings. Patrick had to comb my mane a hundred times, with his left hand tight on my halter and his cheek pressed so firmly against my neck that I could feel the frosty stiffness of his beard.

I heard a click of metal, and then the clap of the gunshot, so loud that it seemed to shatter the air.

I tried to jump away, but Patrick was still holding me tightly. Along the picket line, other ponies leapt and twitched. One of them shrieked and another whinnied, and the gunshot still seemed to ring in the air.

Then I heard the soft thud of Jehu collapsing.

Mr. Atkinson didn't move for a long time. Then he walked toward his pony, passing Mr. Oates, who was walking back, both of them watching their own feet. Mr. Atkinson knelt in the snow and began to unbuckle Jehu's halter. I could feel his despair from all the way across the camp.

That night, the dogs had a feast, which rather turned my stomach. I heard them growl and snap at each other, the dog Osman the loudest of all. I saw blood dripping from his muzzle and his mane, blood on his fangs and paws.

I was glad that Jehu wasn't there to see that.

It was a long, sad rest I had, through the brightest part of the day to the start of the next night's march. I kept thinking of Jehu, remembering how happy he had been to roll in the snow when the ship first arrived. Though I was sorry he was gone, I was even sorrier for the men, and especially for Mr. Oates. He came out by himself while the other men were sleeping, and went from pony to pony just to tighten blankets, pet a nose, or rub an ear. I remembered what he'd said on the ice in the terrible time the year before: "I shall be sick if I have to kill another horse like the last one." He seemed so mixed up inside that I couldn't sort out what he was thinking.

Two of the motor party turned back. Mr. Atkinson stepped into the harness and pulled the sledge that Jehu had pulled.

We saw the mountains to the west as a dark and distant blur. But soon it snowed again and turned our world to white.

That was the last time Chinaman saw the mountains. The blizzard blew without stopping, covering the Barrier in a sludge of soft snow. We all waded through it, men and ponies both. Christopher struggled as much as Chinaman now. Even that big monster of a pony was fading quickly.

For another four days, poor Chinaman struggled on. And they were the hardest days of all. The never-ending gleam of white snow and white sky burned my eyes badly. Snow covered my nose when I walked. It covered my ears and my forelocks, and I had to snort it away from my nostrils. It covered my blanket when I rested. Then it melted. Then it froze, and I felt like a block of ice.

When Mr. Oates led him away, Chinaman didn't even bother to glance up. He was the most worn-out, tired-looking thing I'd ever seen, slumped and sad. I heard him whooshing his slow breaths with his muzzle near the ground while

Mr. Oates prepared the pistol. But at the very end, he lifted his head and looked north down the tracks of our day's march. His ears pricked up, as though he'd heard a sound of happy memories. His tail swished, flinging clumps of snow.

I saw nothing on the Barrier, where Chinaman was looking. But he opened his mouth and made the shrill cry of greeting that I'd heard at Blucher's grave. Then Mr. Oates held out his pistol, the shot boomed, and poor old Thunderbolt fell with a whoof and a thud.

Again the dogs had a feast. And the men, in their tents, cooked up a rich-smelling stew. It made me queasy to think of what they were eating.

Mr. Wright joined the man-haulers. We marched to the south, through blizzard after blizzard.

Captain Scott pressed us on; he had to make his thirteen miles a day. But every march was worse than the one before, and the men grew as tired as the animals. There was deep snow to wade through, and underneath, a crust that sometimes shattered. Patrick broke through it as often as me, his arms and hands sinking into the snow as he fell. Side by side, we staggered and plunged and heaved ourselves on. And no one thought of turning back. That was how badly the captain and the rest ached to reach the Pole; they would never turn back, no matter what.

Every march ended when Captain Scott blew his whistle. It was sharp and loud, like the cry of a hawk, and I came to love that shrill screech more than any sound I'd ever heard.

When the whistle blew, Patrick thumped my neck or patted my nose and told me, "Good work, James Pigg."

My work was over, but my worry began. At the end of every march, I wondered if my end had come. I watched Patrick for a clue as he led me from the trail, as he unfastened my harness. I listened for clues in his voice. And I watched Mr. Oates as closely as I'd watched him on the little island where I'd first seen him. When he bent down to a sledge, or crawled into his tent, or reached a hand in his coat, was he fetching his pistol?

I didn't want to be afraid, but I couldn't help it.

But it wasn't my turn next. It was Christopher's.

The choice was Captain Scott's. Mr. Oates wasn't pleased, and they argued loudly back and forth. Mr. Oates said Christopher was strong enough to go a lot farther, to go right over the Beardmore if he was asked to do it. But Captain Scott said Christopher had been nothing but trouble from the start. And at any rate, he said, his mind was made up.

Mr. Oates led the pony himself. He used one hand to lead his pony, and the other to carry his pistol. Then they stood together in the ruts of the sledges, with Mr. Oates leaning against Christopher.

I wished I could hear what he was saying. But it was all in whispers and murmurs, while his hand went round and round over the shaggy white hair of the pony.

For once in his life, Christopher didn't try to pull his head away, or rear up, or stomp the snow with his hooves. He just stood there, huffing gently, then made a soft nickering sound.

When Mr. Oates brought up his pistol, I didn't want to see what would happen. I looked for Patrick and saw him hurrying toward me, staggering through a drift of snow as though a wolf was right behind him.

Then the shot made me jump. I jerked at my tether. I tried to bolt, and nearly tangled in the picket line. Then Patrick was beside me, and I didn't worry anymore.

My ears rang with the crack of the shot. But still I heard Christopher scream. Then I saw him gallop past, more wild than he had ever been. He kicked and he bucked; he spun in tight circles.

Mr. Oates ran after him with the pistol still in his hand. He had somehow missed his shot.

The men chased Christopher through the camp. They spread out in a line and tried to surround him. Birdie Bowers waved his felt hat in the air.

Christopher shied away from one of the men, only to turn and face another. He was terrified, and the smell of his fear made the rest of the ponies uneasy. The men closed in around him. He ran up against a sledge. He nearly trampled a tent, and all the time kept shrieking and fighting, leaping clear from the ground with his four hooves flailing.

Then a man grabbed his tether. And three others held on while the pony bucked and struggled. But Mr. Oates got him calm again, then led him back to the trail.

They went right past me. I saw a hole in the side of Christopher's head. Drops of blood had been flung in a red spray through the hairs around it. Mr. Oates looked awfully wretched.

I didn't watch where they went. The pistol clicked, then fired again, and the monster was no more.

❄   ❄   ❄

Now there were seven ponies. Again our loads were lightened as the men cached more supplies. Then on we went into the white haze.

It was thick as milk to start with, but it grew thinner as we walked. Patches of sky appeared in the east, then rocky cliffs of yellow and brown. A tumbling glacier shimmered between snow-covered peaks, as blue as the eyes of a sledge dog.

Mr. Wilson shouted, "There's the Gateway!" and I looked straight ahead, and I could hardly believe what I saw.

Below a band of clouds was a snowy ramp leading up through the mountains, up through a river of ice. On either side were pillars of rock, and the clouds seemed to arch across them.

It was my old vision of the ponies' place, the image that I'd seen in the wretched stables long ago. I'd never thought I would actually see it, but now I struggled on toward the Gateway, as though into my own imaginings.

For an hour or more, it was there in front of me, glaring and bright. It encouraged me on, until Patrick had to slow me down because I was pulling him along. High in the mountains, the wind whipped snow from the Beardmore, wild whirls that raced across the surface like the spirits of the glacier. Then the clouds thickened, filling the Gateway, and soon it was snowing again.

I wasn't sure that I would ever reach the Gateway. It was many days in the distance, and I was failing quickly.

It was Victor who trailed at the end of the line that day. He was Birdie Bowers's pony, and the little man trudged beside him, not caring how slowly they walked. They came into the camp together, and Captain Scott went out to meet them.

Birdie seemed surprised at that. He stopped, looked up at Captain Scott, and put his hand on Victor's muzzle, as though to guard the pony.

"He's not doing very well, is he?" asked Captain Scott.

"Oh, he's all right, sir," said Birdie, with a funny little smile. He rubbed harder on the pony's nose. "He's pulling his weight and more."

Captain Scott, in his sledging clothes, looked as big as a bear beside Birdie. His face was windburned, his eyebrows frosted. "It's the end for him, Birdie," he said.

"But, sir—"

"The forage is running out," said Captain Scott. "There's not enough for all the ponies, and I've made up my mind."

"But, sir," said Birdie again. "I told you that. I asked for more, and . . ." He looked away; he couldn't bring himself to argue with the captain. In the end, it would have made no difference.

"I'll send Oates," said Captain Scott, and he turned around and left.

Poor little Birdie Bowers stood and petted his pony. When Mr. Oates came with the pistol, Birdie asked him to wait. Then he got out his own biscuits—his dinner—and fed every one of them to Victor, though it meant he would go hungry himself that night. He broke them into little pieces that he fed to the pony one by one, so that Victor might think he was getting more than he really was.

Mr. Oates didn't try to hurry him. He looked embarrassed as he stood there waiting, examining his pistol over and over, as though it was something he had never seen and couldn't quite understand.

Then the last bit of the last biscuit was gone, and Birdie looked up at Mr. Oates. He had to look up at everyone, poor little Birdie. "Well, I suppose that's it," he said. "Thank you, Oates."

Still, he didn't want to let go of Victor. The pony still seemed strong and healthy to me. He looked back at Birdie as Mr. Oates led him away. Then he trotted along with high steps, as he thought he was heading for a warm stable at last.

I watched Birdie turn away and head toward his tent. It seemed that he was in a hurry to get there. But the roar of the pistol stopped him for a moment. He straightened—looking very tall for a moment—then slumped down and went along on his way.

In the distance, the dogs were coming. Their barks and howls were growing louder.

❄   ❄   ❄

All the way from the winter station, the dogs had carried food for ponies. I had always thought it was a bit funny they would do that. But now it seemed cruel, just the very sort of thing a dog would do. They had made Victor big and fat, and now they threw themselves at the pieces of him.

They ate and they ate until they could eat no more, until the snow was red all around.

For me, there wasn't enough. I was still hungry when I finished my meal, though I snuffled up every last bit from the bottom of my nose bag. Patrick looked at me sadly. "That's all there is. I'm sorry, lad," he said.

Now Mr. Meares had his eyes on *me*, I thought. Three times I saw him looking at me across the camp, past the peak of his tent. I imagined he was measuring in his mind the pounds of flesh I had, calculating how many meals he could find for his horrible dogs. When he came along the line of ponies, petting every one, I cringed from his touch, from the smell of dog on his hands. I felt as though death was touching me.

It was another miserable night. My blanket was sodden from melted snow and sweat, then froze as the sun carried his light far to the north. Patrick came along and tightened it, pulling the icy layers close against my ribs. He was trying his best to help, but he only made me colder.

Then the wind blew hard. It blew harder than ever before. The tents fluttered and banged, the dogs dug themselves deep, and the sledges disappeared under enormous moving drifts. A river of snow seemed to flow across the Barrier. It toppled the pony wall, and icy pellets rattled on our blankets. It nearly knocked me off my feet.

I couldn't look into that wind. So much snow streamed across the Barrier that I could hardly see Nobby beside me. I shivered under my blanket.

But out of the whiteness came Mr. Oates. He was leaning forward, struggling for every step, and behind him came Birdie Bowers and Captain Scott. I saw Cherry, with his glass eyes already balls of snow, and Patrick and all the others. They looked like gray shadows as they set to work in the howl of wind, to rebuild the pony wall.

*　*　*

We marched in breaks between the blizzards. Captain Scott pushed us hard, trying to make his thirteen miles. With skis strapped to his feet, he moved up and down the line as we straggled south together.

On the outside he looked hard as rock—browned and toughened—by wind and sun and weather. But on the inside he was worn away, whittled down like the lonely cairns on the Barrier. He said no man deserved to find winter weather in the middle of summer.

It was as though the place had turned against him, that the mountains—like giants—were trying to blow him right back to the sea. Captain Scott had come with his motor sledges, with his ponies and dogs and men, all marching like an army to conquer the mountains. Maybe they didn't want us on their backs. Maybe the Pole preferred not to be found.

I was no longer in the lead. Again we straggled along, with Bones and Snatcher and Snippets pushing past me. Often Nobby and Michael passed me too, and I was last of all, too far back to see anyone else. It was just me and Patrick plodding through the white mist.

It's October 19 when Amundsen finally starts for the Pole. Now it's spring without doubt, and there's not a thought of turning back. He has no idea how far the Englishmen might have gotten by now, if they've met the same cold that forced him off the Barrier. He thinks of the motor sledges; he imagines their tracks turning round and round, mindless of the temperature.

There are five men and four sledges. There are thirteen dogs to pull each sledge, and they go seventeen miles before they camp. After four days, they're ninety miles nearer to the Pole.

But ahead are the mountains, and the climb to the polar plateau, and no man has even searched for a route from this direction.

Amundsen loads his sledges heavily at his 80-degree depot. He decides to limit his marches to seventeen miles a day until he sees how the dogs cope with the weight. But in the first hour, they cover six and a quarter miles.

On November 6, when Scott is one day out from Corner Camp, Amundsen leaves his last depot at 82 degrees and heads toward the unseen mountains.

"Now the unknown lay before us," he writes. "Now our work began in earnest."

Chapter Eleven

THERE were times when it was beautiful. Behind the clouds, the sun encircled himself with giant rings of different colors, like pale rainbows all around him. They shone through the clouds and onto the snow, and Patrick stopped me once to admire it. We might have been the only creatures in the whole world, with the whiteness all around us. "Now, isn't that a splendid sight, James Pigg?" he asked. The light shimmered above us; it shimmered in front of us, great rings of gold and blue and yellow. Patrick petted my nose. "We might be looking at the eye of God," he said.

And there were times when it was strange. Out in the snow on a windy day, a pony came from behind me. I was plowing through a hollow full of powdery snow, my shoulders aching from the harness. Patrick used my halter to hold himself up as he waded and staggered along. In an hour we'd moved a hundred yards, and I was so tired that I could hardly keep awake. I knew I was right at the back of the line.

The pony came up through the blowing snow without a sound of breaths or hooves or harness. He just appeared beside me and glided past at a steady trot, not even denting the snow with his hooves. He had neither a handler nor a sledge, and moments later, he'd overtaken us and was disappearing into the blizzard. I called out with a shrill whinny that Patrick didn't understand. "Easy, lad," he said. "I know it's hard."

The pony kept moving, fading away. But he turned his head just enough, in the instant before he vanished, that I saw that he was Blucher.

❄   ❄   ❄

Michael's end came next. The small pony with the tiny hooves, the one who ate my fringes, had his nose bag on when Mr. Oates came to fetch him. His handler was Cherry, and I had never seen a man so sad as poor Cherry was just then. He asked Mr. Oates to wait until Michael had finished eating, and that didn't take very long because there wasn't a lot in our feed bags. He petted the little pony every minute. Then he took off the bag and scraped the inside of it for the last flakes that Michael couldn't lick from the folds and the corners. He held them out on his palm, his hand bared to the cold. Then his glass eyes frosted over, and that made him seem like a spirit.

Michael went playfully. He was always happy with Mr. Oates, and he must have imagined that they were off on some sort of game. He rolled in the snow, then sprang to his feet, then nickered with his teeth showing, as though the whole thing was a great joke.

I didn't want to watch him being shot. I muzzled at my feed bag, wishing I didn't have to hear the sounds. I was glad the little pony fell so softly into the snow.

And now there were five of us. We were twelve miles from the Gateway. One more day would get us there, and I didn't know if I should be happy or afraid. Just then, all I felt was loneliness.

When the men were in their tents, and we were shuffling sleeplessly along the picket line, the clouds sailed away and I saw the Beardmore.

It was horrible but beautiful, a hundred miles of ice pouring down between the mountains, shattered by crevasses, jumbled with enormous blocks and ridges. I could see why no pony had ever climbed it. I didn't believe it was possible. The Beardmore looked worse than the Barrier, and all uphill for a hundred miles. I hoped just then that Captain Scott wouldn't even *ask* me to climb it.

The Gateway didn't look so much like a gateway anymore. We were too close; there was no arch of clouds to close it in. The mountains at the sides seemed more like barriers than pillars. My mountains at home had been friendly and safe, but these seemed only cruel.

I felt scared. I felt cold and very alone. I wanted to huddle close to Snatcher or Snippets, but we were spread too far along the picket line. We could only look at one another, and the two of them stared at me with wide and wondering eyes. They looked fearful, trapped somehow on the huge Barrier.

I didn't sleep. I watched for Patrick, staring at his tent for hour after hour.

Clouds moved in again, hiding the Beardmore. Snow began falling, very soft and silent, with huge flakes drifting down. Then the wind picked up again, and the snow became a stinging sleet.

I kept staring at the tent. I could feel half-melted snow slithering from my forelocks, dripping from my mane. I had to blink it away. Everything looked dim and watery.

When Patrick appeared, a blizzard was blowing again. The sides of his tent were booming in the wind, and the pony wall had tumbled.

It was a wretched, awful day. The snow was wet enough to soak through my blanket, until every inch of me was wet. Then the temperature fell, and all the water turned to ice. I shivered so hard that I thought my bones would shatter.

For four days, it was like that. Howling wind and sleet one moment, enormous flakes the next, tumbling through the air like a storm of butterflies.

Mr. Oates stayed with us. He fussed with our blankets and rubbed us down. Then he huddled by himself against the pony wall while the wind whipped over his head. The men kept saying that the temperature was well above zero, but I had never felt so cold.

On the third day, Blossom went by. I saw him only vaguely, through whirls of blowing snow. He walked as though there was no wind, his mane unruffled, his forelock hanging straight. Like Blucher, he stepped along on top of the snow, and he left no tracks on the powdery surface. I remembered him as sickly and old, a staggering thing. But now he looked younger than I'd ever known him, strong and healthy.

He passed between the tent and the pony wall, very close to Mr. Oates and Snatcher. The man didn't see him, but Snatcher did. He turned to look, snow tumbling from his hair as he raised his head. But already Blossom was gone, a faded ghost in the blizzard.

I hadn't slept since the storm began. I was cold and tired. But I was sure that I saw Blossom, unburied from his grave.

An hour later, the wind began to ease. The snowfall stopped, the sky brightened, and the men crawled out from their tents.

They looked like foxes emerging in the spring, wary and worried. Their tents were drifted over so heavily that only the tips of the bamboo poles were poking from great mounds of white. They came out wet and miserable, from a warm dampness to a world of unbelievable snow.

The sledges were buried four feet deep. The dogs couldn't be seen at all, though wisps of steam rose from the little holes where they'd dug themselves in.

The men brought shovels and picks. They dug out the tents; they dug out the sledges. Mr. Oates and Patrick gave us our nose bags, though there was so little food inside them that it was hardly worth the bother.

Patrick offered a biscuit. What an effort to lift my head enough to take it. Cold and wet and frozen, I felt more dead than alive.

As quickly as it had cleared, the sky filled in again. Clouds thick and gray descended on the Barrier, and snow came drifting down.

Captain Scott looked sad and beaten. He had lost four days: He should have been another sixty miles ahead, halfway up the glacier. He couldn't wait any longer to get started again. He asked for Nobby to be led out so he could see how the surface would hold up. Mr. Oates said it was a wasted effort to untie the pony, but the captain insisted.

Nobby looked as tired as me. He dragged his feet through the snow, then sank to his belly as soon as he rounded the end of the pony wall. The fresh drifts were nearly as tall as Mr. Oates.

We couldn't pull our sledges through snow like that. So the men settled down with cups of tea, and all of us waited. And we waited some more.

The coldness came back as the sun swooped toward the Barrier. A crust formed on the snow, and everything froze again. But still we waited. By the time the men had slept and woken, I was desperately hungry. I scraped at the snow to tell Mr. Oates I was looking for food.

Of course he understood. He came and rubbed my neck, trying to stir up a warmth inside me. "There's no more," he said. "Not a handful of forage, not a scrap of oil cake. I'm sorry, James Pigg. It's gone."

I couldn't believe that Captain Scott would make us march without food, or that Mr. Oates would let him. But while the sun was climbing up again behind the clouds, the men got ready for the march.

Traces and harnesses were laid out. The tents were struck and packed onto sledges. The dogs came awake, and for them there was plenty of food.

Patrick fed me another piece of biscuit—just a little scrap. I knew he was offering his own food, but I couldn't help eating it. I gobbled it greedily from his hand. Oh, I felt like a lucky pony, but not so lucky as Nobby. He got every one of Mr. Wilson's biscuits—all five, one after the other. From the look on Mr. Wilson's face, I guessed he was feeding his pony for the very last time.

The snow hadn't frozen. It was still powdery and soft, in most places as deep as a pony's belly. The men had to wear their skis to stay on top of it.

We had a dozen miles to go, and no more food to eat. I wondered if there was a cache of fodder waiting at the Beardmore. Or would that be the end for all of us?

The men led the way. The big sailor Taff Evans and his crew headed off with their sledge, laboring through the drifts. Captain Scott and Birdie Bowers took another, trying to make a trail for the ponies. They hauled their sledges half a mile, then came back without them. "Right. Let's get the ponies moving," said Captain Scott.

Snatcher was first. A crowd of men gathered behind his sledge and pushed it, while Mr. Oates pulled on the tether. Snatcher moved forward. He leapt up in his traces and plunged into snow to his waist. He had to struggle out of the hole he'd made, only to sink into another. The men pushed and pulled and got him moving, then came down the line to help old Bones.

I was the last. I saw Bones get started, and Snippets and Nobby. They looked like sea lions wallowing over waves of snow. It was no easier for the men, already exhausted and covered in white. By the time they reached me, they were sullen. They were silent. I didn't like the feelings that came off them, filling the air like smoke. There was bitterness and anger and dreadful impatience.

A man grabbed my halter. It was the Russian, the dog driver, and it didn't matter to him that Patrick was there already. He just grabbed and pulled. He shouted at me in Russian, commanding me to move.

The one word brought back such terror. I remembered a hundred whippings that had begun with that word, a clubbing that had left me senseless, a bottle breaking on my shoulder.

The man shouted again. He wrenched on my halter.

Patrick pushed his arm away. "You leave him alone," he snapped. "He's my pony. I know how to handle him."

For Patrick, I tried my best. I pulled with every bit of strength I had, while the men pushed the sledge from behind. My traces went slack, and I hurled myself at the harness. The sledge moved along, though it slithered to one side and tried to pull me over. But I kept my balance and struggled down the broken path of ponies and sledges and men.

"Good lad," said Patrick. "Good lad, James Pigg."

I wanted to keep going. But I couldn't. The snow was too deep. I was too hungry, too tired and cold. I took three more steps, then collapsed in the snow.

I dragged Patrick with me. He fell forward and sideways, sprawling out across the snow.

The Russian hit me with a ski stick, a sharp smack across my flanks. It was more shocking than painful, but I shrieked. Patrick roared at the man: "Get away!" Then Captain Scott was there, standing over us on his skis, looking down with his old look of worry and care.

I knew he would end the march right there. He would tell the men to pitch the tents, to rebuild the wall. He would send Mr. Meares with his dogs to fetch the fodder we'd left behind, and we'd eat our fill and everything would be all right. He would make new snowshoes that would hold us up with their magic, and we would glide across the snow as though it was grass and clover.

But he didn't do any of that. He looked down at Patrick and said, quite coldly, "If the animal won't move, you'll have to drive him."

Patrick was on his knees beside me. He looked back at the captain as though he didn't understand.

"Do whatever it takes. Just get him moving," said Captain Scott. "The sooner it's over, the better." He had the points of his sticks resting on his skis, leaning his weight on the handles. "We have to get out of this . . ." He gestured with one of the sticks, sweeping the point in an arc. "This slough of despair."

The Russian grabbed my halter and hauled me up. He twisted on the leather, forcing me backward. "Up! Up!" he shouted in Russian. Patrick looked terribly sad, but he didn't try to stop him. Captain Scott watched with an expression that was more disgust than satisfaction, then turned his skis around and went off along the line.

From ahead came the smack of leather, the frightened squeal of a pony. I saw Snippets trying to leap through the snow, a man lashing his shoulders with a harness strap. The Russian raised his hand and brought the ski stick whistling down onto my back. I struggled up, trying to watch Patrick. But he looked into my eyes for an instant, then turned away.

A *slough of despair*. The captain had the right words exactly. The Barrier was more a bog than a snowfield, and we mired in it, everyone of us. The soft snow dragged us down like quicksand and held us in place as we tried to move forward. It swallowed the sledges until the men had to lever them out. And through the air flew the shouts of men, the sound of ponies screaming.

I saw Mr. Oates strike at Snippets with a tether rope—again and again—as the pony wallowed on his knees. I saw Cherry hitting Bones so hard that his glass eyes were flung askew. And even Patrick lashed me with a tether.

They didn't beat us with the cruel pleasure of my old Russian masters. They didn't leer as they did it. They didn't laugh. But they did it. They hit us; they shouted; they drove us along.

I felt betrayed.

❄ ❄ ❄

For the first time in my life, I wished I was a dog. Maybe Captain Scott wished for it to, because this was a place that was meant for dogs, not for ponies. Everyone knew it, but nobody said it.

For twelve hours we floundered and struggled and plunged

214

through the snow. We didn't stop for lunch; there *was* no lunch. Patrick stuffed a bit of old biscuit in my mouth as I lay trembling in the snow. But he yanked on my tether before I could eat, and it fell out of my mouth as he tugged me forward. When I tried to reach it, he pulled my head around. "Come on. Get up!" he shouted, and someone strapped me from behind. I had to leave the biscuit lying on the snow. It was nibbled around the edges—a people's biscuit—left forever on the Barrier.

The white haze was thick all around us for most of the day. It made shadows of Snatcher and Snippets, with shadow men whipping them on. It made their cries seem softer. Then it cleared very quickly, and I saw them distinct and sharp against the snowy slope of the Gateway. One was lunging at his harness, his sledge half buried. The other had sunk to his belly, and two men were trying to haul him up.

The mountains were close around us, the Beardmore crawling up between them. I thought again that they didn't want us there, that they hated Captain Scott. They had piled the snow in front of him; they had turned the Barrier into a swamp. But still he'd forced us through it, right to the foot of the Gateway.

The surface was hard and windblown there. We stood again on top of the snow, breathless and wheezing. Patrick reached out to pet me. I shied away from the movement, and that put such an awful look in his eyes that I wished I hadn't seen it.

"It's all right. It's over now," he said. He moved his hand more slowly. But still I closed my eyes until I felt his fingers in my forelocks. "You're a good lad, James Pigg," he whispered.

We marched in a ragged line toward the mountain, every pony wheezing, every man hunched over. My shadow walked beside me, our hooves stuck together. It had the long, thin legs of a racehorse, a neck like a swan's, but its ears were as tall as a rabbit's. Patrick's shadow led my shadow, as though four of us walked together.

Right ahead on the blue top of the Beardmore, where it swept to the right between the great pillars of the Gateway, I saw three ponies walking. They weren't the gray and ghostly things I'd seen in the blizzard but sharp little figures high on the ice, white against the blue. They walked on a glaring whiteness, in the warmth of full sunlight, but they had no shadows beside them.

I watched the distant ponies pass beyond the great pillar of rock and ice. Then Captain Scott blew his whistle, and we came to the end of the march. We turned to the left one by one, as we had done so many times before. But the men didn't set to work building a pony wall, and they didn't stretch out a picket line. Captain Scott nodded to Mr. Oates, who went away and got his pistol.

He took Snatcher first. The rest of us stood with our handlers, so tired now that we could barely stand. Patrick kept rubbing my nose. He started talking to me, telling me about all the things we'd seen.

"Do you remember the island?" he asked. "That's the first place I saw you, James Pigg. Where that lady took a fancy to you; do you remember that? She'd be proud to see you now, I think."

I heard the bang of the pistol. Mr. Oates came trudging back for Snippets.

"Then we had that long voyage. Do you remember that?" Patrick sniffed. He wiped his nose with the back of his hand. "You weren't too keen on the sea, were you, lad? That terrible storm; do you remember? I don't mind telling you now, James Pigg. I was badly afraid."

The second shot rang out. Snippets made a sound like a sob as he fell.

Patrick's hand shook as he kept stroking my ears. "You were so happy to get ashore. I remember how you rolled in the snow. And the crevasse; do you remember that?" He half laughed and half sobbed. "We nearly lost you down there."

Mr. Oates took Bones away. The big pony went slowly, a soft snort with each step.

"And there was that time on the ice with the whales all around us," said Patrick. "And all those poor ponies. They called you a crock; but you were never a crock."

There was another shot. Patrick held me firmly, so I couldn't turn my head. By the shaking of his hands, I guessed that old Bones didn't die right away. I heard the thud as he fell, then the scrape of hooves in the snow.

"And the winter. That was a long time for you to stand in a stable," said Patrick. "And you saved my life; do you remember? When we lost our way, you led me back to the hut. Maybe you meant to; I'll never know."

Mr. Oates took Nobby. The pony's handler turned away, the smell of sadness very thick around him.

"You nearly died of the colic." Patrick combed my forelock the way I liked so much. His tears were freezing in the corners of his eyes, making icicles on his cheeks. "I'm sorry," he said. "For all of it. I'm sorry, James Pigg."

I pushed my nose up against him. I made the sound of contentment, but he didn't understand. He thought I was looking for biscuits in the padding of his pockets.

"Oh, lad, I haven't any more," he said. But he felt through his pockets anyway, and he found the smallest crumb of a biscuit, no bigger than a sugar cube.

I licked it from the fingers of his glove. Then I kept licking, enjoying the feel of the wool, all the scents and tastes of the man I loved so much. Behind me, the pistol cracked again. There was another thud, then the sound of Mr. Oates coming to get me.

"Oh, James Pigg." Patrick put his arms around me. He pressed his face against my hair. "I'm going to miss you dearly," he said. "You're such a good lad, James Pigg."

Mr. Oates let me walk as slowly as I liked. He didn't make me hurry at all for my last few yards. He led me near to Snippets and Snatcher and Bones and Nobby, all sprawled out on the snow as though they were sleeping.

The dogs were coming now, running up from the south with a spray of powder flying up from their feet. They made a white haze of their own, half hiding Mr. Meares at the back of the sledge. I heard their barks and howls.

Then Mr. Oates swung me around, and I was facing the Beardmore. It looked again like my old vision of the ponies' place, and I wondered if I'd been right about that. I had come close already to finding the things I'd imagined: a heated stable, blankets made warm by the stove. I had seen men step into the harness and share my load. Men had served me, building walls to keep me sheltered, feeding me biscuits and oil cakes.

Mr. Oates put the end of his gun to my head. I could

see how much he hated doing it, but I couldn't quite sense his feelings. It was as though he had shut them off, or shut them out, and in his mind was only the job of aiming his pistol.

"So long, James Pigg," he said. "If there's a heaven for horses, I'll find my way there." Then he pulled the trigger.

❄ ❄ ❄

I went up the Gateway at a gallop. I flew across the snow like a colt again. In a moment, I was over the summit and hurtling down to the Beardmore. Snow turned to ice under my hooves and I ran along with a clatter, up to the rocky pillars, up to the arch of clouds.

My mane streaming back, my hooves flashing, I rounded the turn in the glacier and saw a huge white plain, and a stable up ahead. It looked warm and rosy-bright inside, with a little chimney wisping smoke, little windows glowing. The snow had melted from the roof and lay in huge mounds below the eaves.

The door swung open as I neared it. I saw Jehu in there, and old Uncle Bill and Hackenschmidt. I heard my mother cry from a line of ponies that seemed to stretch ahead for mile after mile after mile. And I raced over the threshold, onto a floor that was padded with straw.

The ponies all whinnied to greet me.

It's the middle of December of 1911, nearly Midsummer Day in the high south. Captain Scott and his men set up a camp at the foot of the mountains, within a mile of the Gateway.

On the ground lie five dead ponies. They have done their job and soon they'll be butchered. Captain Scott writes in his journal, "Poor beasts! They have done wonderfully well considering the terrible circumstances under which they worked, but yet it is hard to have to kill them so early."

He names the place Shambles Camp.

The men and the dogs go on up the glacier. The storm has covered the ice in thick, fresh snow, the worst conditions that Scott has ever seen. He wishes he could have the luck of Shackleton, who'd found clear blue ice in the same place at the same time of year.

He thinks of Amundsen off to the east. Is the Norwegian suffering under the same conditions? Or do the constant storms blow only against the Englishmen?

After a day and a half of steady climbing, Scott sends back the dogs. From now on, it's nothing but man-hauling, up the long Beardmore and over the polar plateau. The plateau is higher than the Barrier by nearly two miles.

More depots are planted along the way, and men are sent back as their sledges are emptied. Scott writes of the disappointment of men whose hopes for the Pole are dashed forever. At the top of the glacier, it's the end of the trek for Dr. Atkinson and Silas Wright, for Patrick Keohane and Apsley Cherry-Garrard. Just eight men are left, just two teams plodding south, the first led by Scott, the second by Commander Teddy Evans. The second team is tired. On the last day of the year, Commander Evans and his men cache their skis and another hundred pounds of unnecessary gear. The next day, the first of 1912, they rebuild their sledge, making it smaller and lighter. But they still have to struggle to keep up with Scott.

Three days later, the team is sent home. One of the men has come so close to the Pole that he weeps as he turns back.

With a hundred and fifty miles to go, Captain Scott has his polar team. There's his old friend Bill Wilson, the doctor who went with him on Shackleton's expedition. There's the big sailor Taff Evans, the most powerful man on the expedition, who represents "the lower deck," and makes the expedition equal. And there's Lawrence Oates, who did so well with the ponies. From the very beginning, Scott has planned that four men will reach the Pole.

But now, at the last minute, he plucks another from the supporting party. He takes little Birdie Bowers. And five men, harnessed together, pull the last sledge to the south.

Scott is content with his choice. "I think it's going to be all right," he says in his journal. "We have a fine party going forward and arrangements are all going well." But the five men share food that was meant for four. Worst, they're short one pair of skis. Birdie Bowers has to go on foot and struggle to keep up, trotting along in the midst of the group.

On the sixth of January they pass 88 degrees, with a hundred and twenty miles to go. Every hour takes them a mile and a quarter nearer to the Pole, each man moving in silent thought. "What lots of things we think of on these monotonous marches!" writes Scott. "What castles one builds now hopefully that the Pole is ours."

Another day, another march, and they pass beyond the point where Ernest Shackleton turned back in 1909. In his tent that night, within a hundred miles of the Pole, Scott writes in his journal, "I suppose I have made the most southerly camp."

But he can't be certain of that. The question must haunt him: Where is Amundsen? Did the Norwegian find a new route through the mountains? Could his dogs cope with the glacier? Has he turned back, defeated, or is he somewhere up ahead? Has he reached the Pole already?

On the eighth, a blizzard prevents the men from moving on. Dr. Wilson dresses a nasty cut on Evans's hand. Though the wait is frustrating, the men are thankful for a day's rest. It takes all their effort to haul their sledge ten miles in a day, and they have never worked so hard in their lives.

On the fifteenth of January, they make their camp less than thirty miles from the Pole. They plant their last depot, a tiny thing with just four days' worth of food, and set off eagerly in the morning. With twenty miles to go, they stop for lunch, then press on again in high spirits.

Then, not two hours later, Birdie Bowers sees a strange sight.

To him, it looks like a cairn standing out on the plateau. But he isn't sure, and he says it might be a pile of snow, a drift or a wave. Then a black speck appears, and they all know that isn't natural.

They find a flag, and the remains of a camp where the tracks of many dogs, of sledges and skis, are printed in the snow.

"This told us the whole story," writes Scott. "The Norwegians have forestalled us and are first at the Pole. It is a terrible disappointment, and I am very sorry for my loyal companions."

The Englishmen are all feeling the cold. Their hands and feet are frozen. But they go on, of course. The next day, the seventeenth of January, 1912, they reach the South Pole.

This is the day that Scott has been working toward for more than ten years, for the whole of the century. He has planned for it, and dreamed of it, but now he calls it "a horrible day." Amundsen has beaten him. The remains of the Norwegian's camp lie scattered around the Pole, on the frozen wasteland at the very bottom of the world.

"Great God!" writes Scott. "This is an awful place and terrible enough for us to have laboured to it without the reward of priority."

One of Amundsen's tents is still standing. Inside are bags of mitts and sleeping socks and various bits of gear. There is a note dated almost exactly a month earlier, on a day when Scott and his men were still struggling up the Beardmore. It asks Scott to deliver a letter to King Haakon announcing the Norwegians' victory, just in case they don't make it home themselves.

Scott takes the note and leaves his own, a record that he was there, that the Englishmen had reached the Pole.

"We built a cairn," he writes, "put up our poor slighted Union Jack, and photographed ourselves—mighty cold work all of it."

Then they turn to the north, with eight hundred miles of solid dragging ahead of them.

"Good bye to most of the day-dreams," writes Scott in his journal.

Now for the run home and a desperate struggle. "I wonder if we can do it."

At last the wind blows at the backs of the Englishmen. They hoist a sail on their sledge and harness this thing that has caused them so much misery all the way to the Pole.

But the wind is still their enemy. It rises to a blizzard, hiding the tracks that lead to their buried supplies. Soon it will swing around and blow in their faces again.

Scott knows he has pressed his luck. He had planned to be back at One Ton Depot on March 20, at Hut Point a week later. To do it, he has to walk more than six hundred miles in sixty days, and already it's a struggle for the men. Their boots are wearing out; their bodies are wearing out. Oates feels the cold badly in his feet, but Taff Evans is the worst. His hands have never healed and now are badly blistered. There's frostbite on his nose.

Just six days out from the Pole, Scott writes, "Things beginning to look a little serious."

The weather is atrocious. "Blizzards are our bugbear," says Scott, "not only stopping our marches, but the cold damp air takes it out of us."

They plod down their ghostly tracks, following them so exactly that they stumble across small things they had lost on the way to the Pole: a pair of night boots belonging to Evans, mittens that Bowers had dropped, the Soldier's treasured pipe.

It's the end of January now, with temperatures falling. Scott sounds hopeful one day, despairing the next, as he records the failing of his team. Dr. Wilson sprains a tendon and his leg swells up. Two of Taff Evans's fingernails fall away. More troubling, the big sailor is beginning to lose heart.

On February 7, they reach the depot at the top of the Beardmore, only to find that a biscuit tin is missing, a full day's rations vanished. "Bowers is dreadfully disturbed about it," says Scott.

Despite the cold, despite their troubles and their hunger, the men stop along the glacier to collect fossils picked out by Dr. Wilson. They add thirty-five pounds of rock to their sledge.

By the tenth, they have only two days' worth of food remaining, and at least two marches down the glacier to the next depot. And another blizzard is blowing snow across the surface, hiding not only their landmarks but the deep crevasses in the ice. Scott must reduce rations or march blindly if the weather doesn't clear.

They lose their way on the glacier. They think their proper track is off to their left, then off to their right, and they blunder back and forth. That night they think they're on course, but they're not sure. They halve their rations, and are prepared to halve them again if they don't make progress.

"In a critical situation," writes Scott the next day. Their morning march has taken them within sight of an old camp, but the afternoon has found them lost among crevasses and fissures. With one meal remaining, Scott isn't sure they'll reach the next depot.

In fog and haze they wrestle their sledge down the Beardmore.

Evans cries out, "There's the depot!" He thinks he has seen a cairn, but it's only a shadow on the snow. Then, suddenly, Dr. Wilson spots a flag, and the five men have a lunchtime feast at the old depot.

Then it's off again, on toward the next cache on the lower glacier. There's food for three and a half days, and thirty miles to go.

Bowers and Wilson are snow-blind. Oates is bothered by the old wound in his leg. Taff Evans has an enormous blister on his foot, and his mind is beginning to fray.

The snow is soft, the temperature hovering between zero and ten degrees. The men sweat heavily while they work, then freeze when they stop, and their clothes never dry out. Evans slows them down, finding small excuses to halt the march, to get out of his harness and leave the others to do the hauling. He falls behind, then staggers along—alone—trying to catch up.

On February 17, near the foot of the glacier, Evans stops to tie his boots. He asks for a bit of string and says, cheerfully, that he'll be along soon enough. The others go on with the sledge, and when they stop for lunch, they can see the big sailor far behind, plodding through the snow. They pitch their tent, eat their meal. When they look out again, Evans can't be seen.

All four hurry toward him on skis.

"I was first to reach the man," Scott writes the next day, "and shocked at his appearance. He was on his knees with clothing disarranged, hands uncovered and frostbitten, and a wild look in his eyes."

In slow speech, Evans says he thinks that he fainted. The men pull him up, but he falls again. So Oates stays with him while the other three bring the sledge. By the time Evans has been hauled to the tent, he's unconscious. He dies without waking, just after midnight.

Less than half an hour later, the men pack up and move on. They reach their depot, sleep for five hours, then march down through the Gateway to Shambles Camp.

They're back on the Barrier now, with its swampy snow and fragile crust. Their skis and sledge runners leave deep tracks; they can see them for miles behind them. But the old tracks of returning teams are so faint, they're hard to find. Progress is terribly slow. In the Barrier nights, the temperature swings well below zero now. Scott feels winter settling in around them.

Two days' travel brings them to Desolation Camp, where the blizzard had pinned them for four days. They look for buried pony meat but find nothing.

There's a northerly wind that freezes them through and through. But they drag themselves on: five miles in one day, seven in another. On the next, they struggle for eight and a half miles, and Scott writes, "We can't go on like this."

They pass old cairns, old pony walls, worrying that they've lost their way until the next little relic comes into view. They pass a whole camp without seeing it, and when they pitch their camp on the empty Barrier, the thought comes over Scott that he might never find the route again.

It's Bowers's sharp eyes that save them. He sees a crumbling cairn in the distance, and it leads them to the next one, and on to Southern Barrier Depot, where the next disaster greets the men. There's a shortage of oil, which alarms Captain Scott. Returning parties have opened the tins and taken their share. But the leather washers, once disturbed, have allowed the oil to evaporate, and now Scott and his men must ration their fuel.

At the Mid-Barrier Depot, on the first of March, Oates asks Dr. Wilson to look at his feet. The Soldier's toes are very badly frostbitten. He has been marching in agony for the last few days, trying to hide his condition. That's a second blow for Scott, followed immediately by a third. The temperature plummets to forty below and a howling wind covers the Barrier in blowing snow.

At least the wind is from the south. The men hoist the sail on their sledge.

But the surface is so bad that a day's march takes the men only three and a half miles. Their lives depend on reaching the next cache, but it's One Ton Depot that lures them on with its huge stocks of food and fuel. Scott isn't sure they can do it. It's been four months since they left the old hut at the edge of the sea ice, a hundred and twenty nights spent in tents on the Barrier and the Beardmore and the polar plateau. "We are in a very queer street," he writes that night, "since there is no doubt we cannot do the extra marches and feel the cold horribly."

The wind turns again. Blizzards cover the Barrier with woolly crystals that make sledging nearly impossible. The Soldier is lame now, limping in the harness. In grim marches, not five miles a day, they battle on to the next depot, only to find another disappointment: The caches of food and oil are smaller than they're supposed to be. Scott wonders why men have not come out from the huts to replenish the stores, and decides that his dogs must have failed him at last.

It's a sad night for the men. In the morning, on the tenth of March, Oates needs two hours to put on his boots. He asks the doctor what chance he has of reaching Cape Evans, and Wilson says, "I don't know." But to Scott, it's plain. "In point of fact he has none." He writes of Oates's pluck and bravery and says it makes little difference that the Soldier is slowing them down. "With great care we might have a dog's chance, but no more."

There's another blizzard, another march that lasts only half an hour, another cold camp on the Barrier. Then Oates, after breakfast, asks what he should do. The others urge him to go on, but the Soldier knows he's near his end. Scott orders Dr. Wilson to distribute opium and morphine, to give every man the chance to choose his death. Now he notes that the daily distance averages six miles, and he does a bit of calculating in his little notebook:

> We have seven days' food and should be about 55 miles from One Ton Camp tonight, 6 × 7 = 42, leaving us 13 miles short of our distance, even if things get no worse. Meanwhile the season rapidly advances.

But still they press on, over the terrible surface, into the wind, through temperatures of forty below. "Truly awful outside the tent," writes Scott on the fourteenth of March. "Must fight it out to the last biscuit."

At lunch the next day, Oates asks to be left behind. Let him die in his sleeping bag, he says. He doesn't want to be a burden. But the others won't allow it, so he gets up and goes with them, dragging his frozen feet another few miles.

The Soldier goes to sleep hoping that he won't wake. But he does. There's a blizzard outside, shaking the tent, booming in the canvas. Oates crawls from his sleeping bag and unfastens the doorway. "I am just going outside," he says, "and may be some time."

It's too painful for Oates to put on his boots, so he goes out in his socks, into the blizzard. What looks pass between the others?

What words are muttered? Scott says, "We knew that poor Oates was walking to his death, but though we tried to dissuade him, we knew it was the act of a brave man and an English gentleman. We all hope to meet the end with a similar spirit, and assuredly the end is not far."

Now only three men are out on the Barrier. They press on to the north, and pass the eightieth parallel, where Scott had meant to plant his One Ton Depot. If he hadn't turned back to spare the ponies, if he hadn't cared if they'd lived or died, the three men would be wallowing in food that night, their Primus roaring in their tent.

Instead they're dying. Fifteen miles from their cached supplies, they have two days' worth of food. But their feet are getting worse. Scott knows that his will have to be amputated if he ever makes it home.

Another day sees them eleven miles from the depot. But Scott can go no farther. He decides that Bowers and Wilson will press on without him in the morning and return with food and fuel. But they never leave. A blizzard worse than any they've seen blows up in the night, and for a week it never stops.

Birdie Bowers writes a farewell letter to his mother. He assures her that he has struggled on to the end. "Oh how I do feel for you when you hear all," he writes. "You will know that for me the end was peaceful as it is only sleep in the cold."

On March 29, Scott writes in his journal for the final time.

> We had fuel to make two cups of tea apiece and bare food for two days on the 20th. Every day we have been ready to start for our depot 11 miles away, but outside the door of the tent it remains

a scene of whirling drift. I do not think
we can hope for any better things now.
We shall stick it out to the end, but we
are getting weaker, of course, and the
end cannot be far.
It seems a pity, but I do not think I can
write more.
R. Scott

Last entry:
For God's sake look after our people.

*Their camp is not found until summer, when rescuers head out
from Cape Evans. The tent still stands on the Barrier. Inside,
Bowers and Wilson are covered up in their sleeping bags, as though
asleep. Scott has tucked his notebooks under his shoulder and
opened the flaps of his sleeping bag. He has died with his arm
stretched out, touching his old friend, Bill Wilson.*

*The rescuers collapse the tent on top of the men. They build an
enormous cairn to cover it, and mark it all with a cross made of
skis. Then they turn back to Cape Evans, back to tell the world
what has happened. And they leave Scott and Bowers and Wilson
to their long sleep in the cold.*

The Terra Nova *carries the news to New Zealand in February
of 1913. From there it's flashed around the world, and it's met with
shock and sorrow. Kathleen Scott, the captain's wife, is at sea*

when she's told of his death. She's heading for New Zealand to meet him, with no idea that she's been a widow for nearly a year already.

The great prize of first to the Pole has gone to Amundsen. But Scott becomes the real hero of Antarctic exploration. The story of his suffering, of his courage and endurance, inspires the world. England honors his request to look after his people with a memorial fund that raises thirty thousand pounds in the first three days, about six times the annual salary of the English prime minister.

In London, where crowds had cheered the Terra Nova on her way to the south, the great newspaper, The Times, mourns the deaths of Scott and Oates and Wilson and Bowers and Evans:

"No more pathetic and tragic story has ever been unfolded than that of the gallant band of Antarctic explorers whose unavailing heroism now fills the public mind with mingled grief and admiration."

On the twenty-first of May, eight thousand people fill the fabulous Albert Hall to hear a talk by Commander Teddy Evans. With him on the stage are many of Scott's explorers, including Mr. Meares and Mr. Ponting, Gran and Cherry-Garrard and Dr. Atkinson. In the audience are Kathleen Scott—now Lady Scott—and the mothers and the widows of the men who sleep in the Barrier's cold.

As Ponting's photographs flash up on a great screen behind him, Evans tells the story of Scott's expedition. He speaks of the first southern journey, when depots were laid across the Barrier. He tells how the dog team driven by Scott and Meares broke through a bridge of snow and plummeted into a crevasse.

Then he talks about the ponies.

In this magnificent hall in the middle of London, below its dome of iron and glass, eight thousand people sit silent in their seats. The man who had steered the Terra Nova south, who had walked with little Blossom across the Barrier, now stands in front of them, talking of ponies that had been taken from Russia and Manchuria and led nearly all the way to the South Pole.

Evans talks of the ordeal on the drifting ice, when the men could not save Uncle Bill or Punch or Guts. He tells how Blucher and Blossom and James Pigg became known as "the Baltic fleet" because they were old and slow. He says Mr. Oates predicted that not one of the three would make it back to the winter station.

The pictures of the ponies are enormous on the screen. There's Blossom; there's Blucher; there's James Pigg staring into the camera.

The commander describes the deaths of Blucher and Blossom, the events he'd seen himself. Then he tells how one little pony surprised them all with his strength and spirit.

"James Pigg," he says, "was a plucky little animal."

Cast of Characters

THE PONIES
(LISTED IN ORDER OF THEIR DEATHS)

Davy and Jones: probably named after their deaths; died at sea

Blucher: old and tired; died coming back from One Ton Depot

Blossom: one of "the Baltic Fleet"; died at the end of the depot journey

Weary Willy: the lazy pony; died near Safety Camp

Guts: a powerful pony; fell through the ice and vanished

Punch: always obedient; died while crossing the ice floes

Uncle Bill: the biggest pony; died on the ice floes

Hackenschmidt: the pony who could not be tamed; died at the winter station

Jehu: the ancient one; died on the polar journey

Chinaman: the stubborn pony; died on the polar journey

Christopher: never tamed; died on the polar journey

Victor: the favorite of Birdie Bowers; died on the polar journey

Michael: the playful little pony; died on the polar journey

Snatcher: strong and steady; died at Shambles Camp, below the Beardmore

Snippets: the nibbler; died at Shambles Camp

Bones: a "flier"; died at Shambles Camp

Nobby: led at times by Captain Scott; died at Shambles Camp

James Pigg: the Winter Pony; died at the foot of the Gateway

THE PEOPLE
OFFICERS

Captain Robert Falcon Scott: leader

Lieutenant Edward "Teddy" Evans: in command of the *Terra Nova*

Lieutenant Henry Bowers: in charge of stores

Captain Lawrence "Titus" Oates: in charge of ponies

Edward Atkinson: surgeon

SCIENTIFIC STAFF

Apsley Cherry-Garrard: zoologist

Tryggve Gran: ski instructor

Cecil Meares: in charge of dogs

Herbert Ponting: photographer

Edward "Bill" Wilson: zoologist, chief of scientific staff

Charles "Silas" Wright: physicist

THE MEN

Thomas Crean: petty officer, Royal Navy

Edgar "Taff" Evans: petty officer, Royal Navy

Robert Forde: petty officer, Royal Navy

Patrick Keohane: petty officer, Royal Navy

Author's Note

I learned the story of Captain Scott when I was a young boy. My father made sure of it. As a young boy himself, growing up in Cambridge, England, he had become an explorer of sorts, wandering through the storerooms of Cambridge University, discovering artifacts and photographs of polar expeditions.

Scott was my father's hero, and so he was mine.

I knew about Lawrence Oates going out into a blizzard on his thirty-second birthday, to die by himself in the hope of saving the others. I knew about the big sailor Taff Evans slowly collapsing, and the little marine—Birdie Bowers—sticking it out to the end. I admired them all. And I loathed Roald Amundsen, the Norwegian scoundrel who had kept his plans a secret so that he might dash to the Pole ahead of the Englishmen. He had stolen their triumph, but not their glory.

In my father's big blue books—the journals of Scott—I saw pictures that Dr. Wilson had painted in the sunless winter at Cape Evans. I saw a copied page from Scott's journal, the desperate handwriting of a man who was dying.

So I must have seen the ponies, white and sturdy, pulling the sledges south. But I don't remember that. And I don't know if I even wondered what happened to them in the end.

I only found out last year, when I took an old book about Scott on a camping trip. I realized that I had never read his story myself, that everything I knew I had learned from my father.

In the book was a photograph of a pony named James Pigg, with a little anecdote about the day he fell into a crevasse on the Barrier. He was saved only because the men had made him roundly fat with all his little treats. He fell until his belly hit the snow, then jammed in the crack like a cork in a bottle.

Right away I wanted to tell James Pigg's story. I thought that it would be warmhearted and fun; if I had known how sad it would turn out to be, I might not have started.

I found it hard to write about all the deaths of all the men. But it was even harder to write about the ponies. I became more attached to James Pigg than to any character I'd ever known. He was like a child, I suppose—taken along without a say and never offered a choice, dependent on the men for everything, convinced they would never hurt him. His last day was so miserable that I thought of inventing a different ending. But that wouldn't have been fair to poor Jimmy Pigg. I wanted more than anything for the story to be true, and I had already strayed here and there from the facts.

The pony's early life is pure invention, of course. The way

that he comes to join Scott is simplified for the story. But after that, everything that he talks about is true, though it didn't always happen exactly as he says. Because the real James Pigg did not see every part of the expedition, I thought it was all right for him to *imagine* that he did. A pony's memories, I decided, can be a bit unreliable. There are four places where the truth is muddled.

Killer whales really did break through the ice, trying to snatch away the dogs. They nearly got Mr. Ponting—the photographer—but not James Pigg.

Captain Scott really did see his dog team plunge into a crevasse. The snow suddenly opened ahead of him, and most of the team sank through it. The lead dog was Osman, and he planted his feet on the far side of the crevasse, just as it says in the story. And Captain Scott really did rescue the dogs by going down through the ice on a rope. But James Pigg was not there to see it. He did not save the dog.

Three ponies really did come to their end as they tried to cross the sea ice. Guts and Punch and Uncle Bill died exactly as described in the story. But James Pigg was taken on a different route by Patrick Keohane, and saw none of these events.

The men really did exercise the ponies through the long black winter by leading them to a remote weather station. But it was Apsley Cherry-Garrard and Birdie Bowers who lost their way back to the hut until they stumbled onto a familiar landmark. James Pigg wasn't with them, and I only imagined that ponies steered the men.

❄ ❄ ❄

By the time I finished *The Winter Pony*, my impression of Scott had changed. I admired him a little less, and Amundsen a lot more. I realized that it wasn't just good luck and bad manners that let the Norwegians triumph.

It was sad to see that, but not really surprising.

For sixty years after Scott's death, he was a great hero: Amundsen was a scoundrel. Oh, there were people who whispered a different story, but nobody listened. Statues went up, books were written, movies were made, and every one of them praised the Englishman.

Then in 1979 a book came out that changed all that. It attacked Scott at every turn, accusing him of countless errors and oversights, blaming him for the deaths of his men. When Scott's journals told of doubts and regrets, they were a faithful record. When they spoke of bravery, of heroism, they were just a pack of lies. Altogether, it was an excellent book, but I don't want to name it, I was so annoyed by the writer. He was like the old archaeologists who opened ancient tombs for others to plunder. The writers who came after him chipped away pieces of Scott's reputation.

It seems a shame, really. The story of Scott is a tale of obsession, of courage and sacrifice. It's one of the greatest ever lived, and Scott is still my hero.

So I hope this story doesn't make people hate him, or assess him too harshly. While it seems very wrong to treat ponies like walking sacks of dog food, it isn't fair to judge the past by modern standards. Scott was nothing if not kind to his ponies. I believe it was that very kindness—his reluctance to push the animals too hard in the first year of his expedition—that killed him.

If he hadn't worried about Weary Willy and the others, his huge cache of supplies at One Ton Depot would have been placed at eighty degrees south latitude. Instead, it was thirty miles north of there, thirty miles farther from the Pole. He knew he was taking a chance but was loath to lose the ponies.

On the long struggle home from the Pole, in the second year of the expedition, Scott passed that more southern point of eighty degrees. But he never reached the second one. He died eleven miles from One Ton Depot. He had lost his wager—the lives of five men against the lives of five ponies.

In his last lonely camp on the Barrier, Scott wrote a letter to the public. Their donations had paid for his expedition, and he wanted to explain why Amundsen had beaten him, why he and four others would never get home.

"We took risks," he wrote. "We knew we took them; things have come out against us, and therefore we have no cause for complaint, but bow to the will of Providence, determined still to do our best to the last.

"Had we lived, I should have had a tale to tell of the hardihood, endurance, and courage of my companions which would have stirred the heart of every Englishman. These rough notes and our dead bodies must tell the tale."

He is still there today, sealed in his tent and buried in snow. Side by side with Birdie Bowers and Bill Wilson, he shuffles along in the moving ice of the Barrier, every year coming inches closer to the tumbling edge at the ocean.

The body of Titus Oates is somewhere behind him, never recovered. A bit farther along lies Taff Evans, both following Scott in their cold sleep. And the bones of the ponies move along with them.

On that great shelf of ice, nothing lasts forever. One day, the whole thing may be gone. But in the sky above the Barrier are points of navigation that never move at all. They're used by pilots to track their courses across Antarctica. And in 2010, those points were named in honor of the ponies and dogs that served in man's race to the South Pole.

Now five of Scott's ponies are remembered forever as points in the sky. There's Snippets and Bones and Jehu and Nobby. And there's Jimmy Pigg as well.

I think it's a beautiful tribute.

Acknowledgments

It took Captain Scott a year and a half to travel from England to the South Pole. It took me a year and a half to write about it.

Captain Scott battled storms at sea, killer whales and calving glaciers, crushing ice and gaping crevasses, frostbite and hunger and blinding blizzards. I got cold one day and put on a sweater.

I can only imagine the ordeals that were faced by Captain Scott. But, like him, I relied on others to get where I was going.

As usual, the first person I called on was Kathleen Larkin of the Prince Rupert Library. She helped me with photographs and horseshoes and the thinking of ponies. She wrote to the

Scott Polar Research Institute in Cambridge, England, which answered many questions about Scott's little ponies.

The next was my father. He had taught me about Scott when I was a boy, and was delighted to hear that I wanted to write about the man who had always been his hero. He took it upon himself, in his eighty-ninth year, to go through the two volumes of Scott's published journals and note every reference to the pony named James Pigg. He lent me books he's owned for more than fifty years, big thick books with big thick pages, so treasured that I was scared to open them.

To understand horses, I turned to my fourteen-year-old niece, Shauna Wells. She gave me a small library of horse stories, and explained with great patience why James Pigg might have done the things he'd done a hundred years before. A lot of others helped me with questions about horses, including Kelly Berthelot, Lillian Kuehl, Tom and Kerry Marcus, and Thomas Uhlig.

For the story itself, I relied, as I always do, on my editor, Françoise Bui, and on my agents, Danielle Egan-Miller and Joanna Mackenzie. They set me off on the right course and warned me if I was going astray. As problems arose, I talked them over with my partner, Kristin Miller, and my old friend Bruce Wishart.

The sadness of the story often wore me down. Many people picked me up again without even knowing it, often with just a smile or a kind word. They include my brothers and my sister, my friends on Gabriola Island, and those both up and down the coast. To all of them, and to those named here, I extend my very deepest thanks.

ABOUT THE AUTHOR

IAIN LAWRENCE studied journalism in Vancouver, British Columbia, and worked for small newspapers in the northern part of the province. He settled on the coast, in the port city of Prince Rupert; he now lives on the Gulf Islands. His previous novels include *The Giant-Slayer*, *The Séance*, *Gemini Summer*, *B for Buster*, *Lord of the Nutcracker Men*, *Ghost Boy*, and *The Lightkeeper's Daughter*. He is also the author of the Curse of the Jolly Stone trilogy—*The Convicts*, *The Cannibals*, and *The Castaways*—and the High Seas trilogy—*The Wreckers*, *The Smugglers*, and *The Buccaneers*.